Marked for Harvest

by

Melissa Kendall

Marked for Harvest

Cover Art by *Kristian Norris*

The Wild Rose Press, Inc.
PO Box 708
Adams Basin, NY 14410-0708
Visit us at www.thewildrosepress.com

Publishing History
First Edition, 2022
Trade Paperback ISBN 978-1-5092-4570-3
Digital ISBN 978-1-5092-4571-0

Published in the United States of America

Her neck tingled, and then, with a sound like rushing water, the snake faded from the woman's shoulders. A sharp pinch told her the shade had materialized on her chest. She peeked beneath her shirt to see a slitted snout staring up at her. The snake's mottled yellow and white body was curled into a heap with only the tip of its triangular-shaped head peeking out from the folds.

The snake flicked its tongue at her. Its memories itched at the back of her mind, but as she mentally reached for them, they squirmed away. She tried again, stretching herself thin, hoping to feel some flicker of intelligence, and found a wisp, the last remnants of the soul's consciousness. She grasped onto it and was catapulted into a memory.

"Please! No!"

Hands clasped like iron bands around her neck and pushed her face-first into the pool. The murky water flooded her mouth and burned in her lungs. She fought, kicking against her assailant, but the cold sapped her strength and burned her eyes.

Through the rippling water, her attacker grinned.

The memory dissolved like sand blowing in the wind, and Elena gasped with recognition. She touched the snake's head with her fingers and sniffed.

"I'm so sorry, Chloe."

Dedication

To Tatiana

Chapter 1

Elena Cain clutched her balled-up clothes and tiptoed across the hardwood floor. Liam, the handsome guitarist she'd met the previous night, was splayed on his stomach on the creaky bed in the corner, a threadbare gray blanket thrown across his legs. Despite the enormous quantity of tequila they'd consumed, he'd brought her to climax several times before collapsing into a drunken stupor.

So, this is my life now. An endless string of one-night stands.

She'd had a chance at love, once. Before life had gotten in the way. She remembered fixing her gaze on the road until her eyes burned from strain, bouncing her knee until her bladder ached. Passing gas station after gas station until the car sputtered to a stop three miles outside Chicago city limits.

Abandoning the only man who had ever truly cared about her.

Sebastian.

She'd never stopped dreaming of him. When times got tough, it was memories of their time together she fell back on to remind herself that life was worth living.

She found a relatively clean patch of floor and shrugged on her bra and panties, keeping one eye on the man in the bed. Although she had seen no ink on him during their lovemaking, she'd been spectacularly drunk.

Liam grunted and flipped over, revealing a neon pink pig tattooed on his stomach. She froze, gaze fixed on the spot, shoulders tensed, but the pig only stared for several long seconds before trotting down the man's torso and vanishing beneath the blanket.

She hastily shimmied into her tight-fitting black dress, twisted her long black hair into a ponytail, and was digging through a pile of crumpled T-shirts on the floor, looking for her wallet, when the pins-and-needles sensation started in her right hand. She checked her palm, and there it was—pink body, beady black eyes, curled tail, and all.

Fine. But don't try anything.

The pig blinked as if to protest its innocence.

"Leaving so soon?" Liam asked. He had thrown the blanket off his legs and rolled to face her.

She clenched her hand reflexively before relaxing it. It wasn't as if he could see the pig, anyway.

"Thanks, but I have to get home," she said. As nice as their time together had been, she didn't want to pick up any more shades. Although mostly harmless, each was a drain on her already slim reserves.

She hurried out of the apartment, closing the door softly. When she turned, an old woman stood at the end of the hallway. Her shock white hair was tied in a severe bun, her wrinkled hands clutched an ebony cane, and her eyes were pools of black tar. She grinned, revealing a mouthful of sharpened teeth.

"Hello, dearest," the woman said in a grating, masculine voice.

Elena shuffled backward until she hit a wall, then searched for the elevator button and slammed her index finger on it repeatedly.

"Such a clever girl," the old woman said. "Doubling back on your trail like that. But now that we're reacquainted," the woman lurched forward, but the door to 205 opened, and a tall man wearing a sleek black raincoat stepped out. When he closed the door, the old woman was gone.

Elena abandoned the elevator and took the stairs to the main floor. When she entered the foyer, chest heaving, there was a young boy with blonde curls and pitch-black eyes standing in her path.

"Running away already?" the shade asked through the boy's mouth. "So rude. At least give me a taste."

"Leave me alone."

The tickling in her hands returned, accompanied by pressure filling her head like an inflating balloon. She held her breath and mentally pushed back on the encroaching presence, but alcohol and lack of sleep had worn her defenses thin. With a sound like tearing paper, the shade thrust her consciousness into the dark void. She could still see the marble floors and silver elevator doors of the entryway, but it was hazy, like looking through a pane of frosted glass.

The shade possessing her body dug through her pockets, found her phone, and used her fingerprint to unlock the device. It dialed a number, then the phone rang three times before a young female voice answered. "Hello?"

"Hi, Wendy," the shade said through her mouth. "You thought you'd never hear from me again, didn't you?"

"Huh?" The voice warbled.

"I just wanted you to know I haven't forgotten you," the shade said. "We'll be seeing each other again very soon."

"T-this isn't funny," the voice sobbed. "Don't call me again!"

The line disconnected.

The shade's rage washed over Elena. It made her dizzy, like wearing someone else's glasses. She thrashed against the restraints, but the shade was too strong, and her world dissolved.

He closed his gloved hands tightly around the whore's neck, silencing her incessant squawking. Her once-blonde hair was blackened with soot and mud, her right eye swollen shut. Blood trickled from her nose and dripped onto his wrist.

She squirmed beneath him, kicking with her bare feet and thrashing from side to side, but he held on tight, adjusting his grip until he found the perfect pressure to keep her gasping without knocking her out.

Her jerking movements weakened and then stilled.

Elena twisted out of the memory, unwilling to experience any more. How had the bastard found her so quickly? She'd been careful, changing her appearance, zigzagging across the state, and keeping a low profile. But it didn't seem to matter how far or how fast she ran. The Harvester always caught up with her.

Cackling laughter echoed in her ears, then the pressure in her head deflated, and she was sucked back into her body in the now-empty foyer. Her rubbery legs buckled, and she braced herself against the wall. When her arms had stopped trembling, she checked her hand and felt a twinge of remorse that the pig was gone.

That was what made the Harvester so dangerous. It jumped between hosts, consuming shades and growing ever more powerful. Eventually, it would tire of their game, and then she would be royally screwed.

She pushed away from the wall. The important thing was to get back to her apartment before another shade took advantage of her weakened state. She exited the building and fast-walked ten blocks until she was back within the safety of her apartment. Then she leaned against the door and looked at a framed photo on the wall. In the picture, a tall woman with dark hair smiled and waved at the camera from atop an oversized picnic chair.

How did you do this for so long, mom? How did you find the strength to keep fighting?

Her mother's soft voice trickled into her mind, humming a familiar melody. A powerful wave of homesickness washed over her.

Thump

Something heavy hit the door, rattling the security chain.

Thump

She hooked a chair from the hall with the tip of her shoe, edging it closer.

Thump

The chair clattered to the ground. She cursed and let go of the door for a split second to grab the chair and fit it against the handle. The door rattled once more, then stilled.

She resisted the urge to scream. Instead, she pulled out her phone and dialed a number with shaking fingers.

A voice thick with sleep answered. "Hello?"

Elena's shoulders relaxed. "Hey, Aunt Martha, it's me."

"Hello dear! How are you?"

"I've, uh, I've been better."

A long squeal, like nails scraping against glass.

Thump

The chair lodged under the door shifted but held.

Her aunt's voice rose. "What was that?"

Elena's mouth dried. She swallowed, but it didn't help. Pressure built at the back of her eyes as she slid down the wall. "It's found me."

"Already?" A gusty exhale. "You can't keep running, dear. Come home. Let us help you."

"No," Elena said quickly. "Anything but that."

After leaving Stillwood, she'd spent several years living with her aunt, if such a life could even be called living. Unlike her mother, Aunt Martha held the belief that the only way for the gifted women of their bloodline to remain safe was to sequester themselves from the outside world.

Might as well join a convent.

It hadn't been all bad, of course. She had occupied those long, boring years scouring her aunt's impressive collection of occult tomes, learning about her gift, and searching for a way to defeat the monster that had taken her mother.

"There must be something else," Elena said. "Can you check the archives? Maybe I missed something."

"Well, I suppose—"

The line disconnected.

Elena looked at her phone, then dialed again, but it only rang and rang without connecting. Eventually, she gave up and shoved her phone back into her pocket.

The sound in the hallway had stopped, at least.

She buried her head in her arms and wriggled her fingers and toes to chase away the numbness settling on her like a chilly blanket. She confirmed the chair was still in place, rubbed away her tears, stripped off her dusty clothes, and dumped them in a hamper. When she was in the shower, with the water coursing down her body, the tension of the day faded away. She stood in the stream until the hot water ran out, then wrapped a towel around her body and returned to the kitchen, intent on trying her aunt's number again. Even though she refused to accept her aunt's protection, she needed help. Her best bet to lose the Harvester was to leave town immediately, which meant she needed money.

The line connected, and a robotic voice said, "The number you are calling is out of service."

I don't have time for this.

It wouldn't take long for the Harvester to regroup, and she had to be out of town before that happened. She scrolled through her contacts, tapped a name, then waited as the phone rang.

"Smythe and Ernest," a cheerful woman said.

"Hi, I'm a client of David Smythe," Elena said. "I need to talk to him." She paused, then added, "It's important."

"Hold please."

"Wait," Elena said, but it was too late. A gentle melody played on her speaker. Three soothing songs later, the line clicked, and a male voice spoke. "Hello?"

"David, hi, it's me." She shot a glance at the door. "I need your help again."

A sigh from the other end. "Elena, I'm not your piggy bank. Now, if are interested in liquidating assets…"

She gritted her teeth. "That's your angle, is it?"

There was one thing her mother had left her that could help. As much as she had been avoiding returning to Stillwood, it wasn't as if she had any other choice.

I'm sorry, mom.

"Fine," she said. "I'll sell the damn house."

"I'll leave the keys in the mailbox," David said. "The place is in decent shape. A local real estate agent checks on it once a week."

She said goodbye, hung up, then threw open the hallway closet and grabbed the bag inside. Then with a final, longing glance at her cozy apartment, she slid the window open to the back lane and stepped onto the grated metal fire escape.

She was halfway down when glass shattered above her, followed by the tinkling sound of shards falling onto metal. She looked up and through the grating spotted a hulking, human-like shape crawling out her window.

She grasped the edge of the railing and vaulted over. She landed waist deep in a pile of garbage, kicked herself free, and shot out of the alley as fast as her legs could carry her.

****

Elena slammed the door of her car and shielded her eyes with her fingers. The old, craftsman-style house perched at the top of a small ridge, draped with green vines as if born from the earth.

Her childhood home and the only thing of value she had left.

Gravel crushed underfoot as she approached the steps curving up the hill, carved into the earth, set with wooden logs at even intervals like keys of a great piano. She walked with care, her feet sliding on the weather-worn ground. After Chloe broke her arm one winter, her mother had declared the steps off-limits.

It hadn't stopped the girls.

She treasured the memories of taking steps two at a time, laughing as she or Chloe fell and tumbled to rest, breathless, at the base of the hill.

And then there was Sebastian.

The thought of seeing him again sent little waves of pleasure rippling up from her stomach.

Get over it. He probably moved away years ago.

She arrived at the top of the hill and winced at the state of the building. Decent shape, David had said. The man was an eternal optimist. Gaps in stucco showed plastic sheeting beaded with moisture. Vines blanketed the house. Someone had boarded up two smashed-in windows on the main floor with plywood.

It was worse than she'd expected but better than she'd feared.

Unfortunately, she didn't have the time or money to invest in repairs. At least the house was worth far less than the land.

It'll be enough. It has to be enough.

Selling the house would be hard, like giving up a piece of her past, but she had no choice. She had to get back on the road before the Harvester found her.

Tension squeezed around her like a vice, forcing her to take shallow breaths. She stared at the steps leading to the front entrance, then crouched. The undersides were rotten. She walked around the porch and vaulted over the railing in a single smooth motion.

She smiled. "Still got it."

A crow fluttered across her path and landed on the railing. It squawked at her.

"What do you want?" She stuck out her tongue.

The bird nodded its head and fluffed its feathers.

"Yeah, yeah. You've had your run of the place, but

that ends now."

She stepped over another rotted board and dug the keys from her pocket, fanning them in her hand. Front door, back door, shed. Two copies of each. David had labeled them, but the labels had peeled off in her pocket, leaving her with a half-dozen options.

She selected a key at random and placed her palm on the door.

It swung open.

"Hello?" she called.

She walked inside, hesitated, then locked the door behind her. Less for security and more to avoid unannounced visitors. She'd left her car as close to the trees as she could so it wouldn't be seen from the street, but there was always the risk a neighbor would spot it and stop by to say hello.

A soft thud came from inside the house. Scenarios flitted through her mind, none of them good. She palmed the keys between her fingers like claws and tucked her fist behind her back.

"Hello? Is anyone here?"

When there was no response, she took a cautious step forward.

Another sound, like a moan. She raised her foot, then stepped down on the same spot. The wood groaned as it flexed. She laughed at her own skittishness. Next, she'd be jumping at shadows.

She avoided the hallway and the closet that still gave her nightmares and tossed her keys on the island countertop. She remembered her mother dressed in overalls, patching a hole she had made in the wall after attempting to play baseball indoors. A stubborn woman with a bright smile before the shades had corrupted her beyond recognition.

While her heart wallowed in the past, her traitorous mind was already three steps ahead. Furniture could go to O'Connor's Auction House, two towns over. For a hefty commission, he'd be willing to send a truck to pick everything up. Artwork would go into storage as its value was sentimental. She'd need boxes and garbage bags to gather clothing and personal possessions to donate to local charities.

As soon as she found a real estate agent to handle the sale and signed whatever forms they required, she'd be back on the road. It would mean living lean for a while, but she was used to that.

Then a flash of movement drew her gaze to the back of the house, where a sliding glass door exited out to the deck.

She walked closer and made out a shape bobbing in the rippling water of the in-ground pool.

She grasped at the door frame.

A woman in an apricot-colored sundress floated face-down in the water, hair fanned about her like a shroud.

Elena forced the air out of her lungs. It couldn't be a body. There had to be some other explanation. She slid the door open, and the cool fall air whipped her hair, bringing with it the distinctive smell of decay.

Her knees wobbled.

Who was she? What was she doing here?

A writhing shape faded into view on the woman's bare shoulders, large and yellow, a snake. She'd seen another like it in the flesh years ago, visiting a zoo with her mother. A friendly keeper had asked if she'd wanted to take a picture with a boa constrictor, and she'd agreed, hanging onto her mother's skirts. The man had loaded the snake onto her shoulders, where it had hung like a dead weight, its chubby body smooth despite the scales.

Her neck tingled, and then, with a sound like rushing water, the snake faded from the woman's shoulders. A sharp pinch told her the shade had materialized on her chest. She peeked beneath her shirt to see a slitted snout staring up at her. The snake's mottled yellow and white body was curled into a heap with only the tip of its triangular-shaped head peeking out from the folds.

The snake flicked its tongue at her. Its memories itched at the back of her mind, but as she mentally reached for them, they squirmed away. She tried again, stretching herself thin, hoping to feel some flicker of intelligence, and found a wisp, the last remnants of the soul's consciousness. She grasped onto it and was catapulted into a memory.

"Please! No!"

Hands clasped like iron bands around her neck and pushed her face-first into the pool. The murky water flooded her mouth and burned in her lungs. She fought, kicking against her assailant, but the cold sapped her strength and burned her eyes.

Through the rippling water, her attacker grinned.

The memory dissolved like sand blowing in the wind, and Elena gasped with recognition. She touched the snake's head with her fingers and sniffed.

"I'm so sorry, Chloe."

She rubbed away the tears on her cheeks and was about to cross the deck when she heard the unmistakable sound of a key turning in a lock.

She closed the sliding door with a soft click and crouched under the kitchen window, back pressed to the stucco exterior of the house.

Be quiet. Don't let them know you're here.

"Hello?" A man's voice, low and rumbling.

Footsteps approached, then stilled.

She inched up and peeked through the window. The man's back was to her. He was tall, with tawny brown hair and deeply tanned skin. He crossed his arms, his shirt tight enough to show off wide shoulders and a narrow waist.

She focused on a splash of emerald on the man's neck. It was another shade, a green tree python. She caught only glimpses of it coiled around the man's shoulders beneath his shirt like the branch of a large tree.

Her fingers were numb because they were clenched so hard.

I have to get out of here.

She looked around the backyard. The cultivated landscaping of her childhood was a chaos of overgrown plants and weeds. She could sprint for the fence, but the windows in the kitchen gave a clear view of that path.

Maybe if she waited, he would leave?

The man turned, and Elena's heart fluttered. He was stunning, with long, dark eyelashes and high cheekbones dusted with stubble. His wide lips thinned as he searched the room, heavy eyebrows drawn close together. It had been years since she'd seen him last, but she recognized him at once, and his name left her lips before she could claw it back.

"Sebastian?"

Chapter 2

Sebastian Castillo couldn't believe his eyes. Standing on the deck was the woman who had shattered his heart into a thousand pieces.

Her face was pinched, her cheeks flushed with color, her lips drawn thin. Her once unmanageable, frizzy brown hair fell down her back in a smooth waterfall of inky black.

"What are you doing here?" he asked, although what he really wanted was to shove his hands into her lush hair, draw her close, and kiss her senseless. Years spent rooting all traces of affection from his heart, and with a single glance, she brought it all rushing back.

Focus. You're here for a reason.

His sister had left a cryptic note on his windshield asking to meet at the house, and he had to find her and stop her before she did something she would regret.

Elena glanced to the side, and he followed her gaze to the pool.

To the body floating in the pool.

"Chloe!"

He burst into movement, sprinting across the deck and descending the stairs three steps at a time. His vision narrowed to the task at hand. He missed the first paving stone and slipped on the gravel that made up the walkway from the deck to the pool. He hit the ground hard, then scrambled to his feet, ignoring the pebbles embedded in his palms.

"I'm coming, Chloe. Hang on!" His voice broke on a sob.

So close now. Only a few more steps.

He stopped at the edge of the pool and dove into the icy water. The resulting wave pushed Chloe out of his grasp. He grabbed her arm and hauled her to the surface.

That's when the smell hit him. A powerful stench that burned the last ounce of hope from his heart.

He turned her over and his mouth filled with a sick-sour tang at how wrong she looked. Her eyes were cloudy, her skin had a blue cast, and her makeup was smeared like she'd been crying. She stared up at him in unblinking accusation as if to say, *why didn't you help me? Where were you when I needed you?*

His throat tightened. He pushed a lock of hair from his sister's face and cupped her frozen cheek in his hand.

"Why didn't you wait for me?"

Her dead body provided no answers.

He hugged her, then took a staggering breath and tugged her to the edge of the pool, where Elena waited. When she saw Chloe's face, she moaned and pressed her fists to her face.

"Help me get her out of here," he said.

They grasped Chloe's arms and legs and lifted her onto the pavement.

Seeing her on the ground was almost worse. She was covered in leaves and flecks of algae, and her dress was hiked up past her knees. He tugged the garment back into place, covering a jagged scar on her thigh.

He remembered the day she got it with startling clarity. He'd left the house after an argument with his parents to go to his usual smoking spot at the base of an old deer stand, deep in the woods. Stewing with anger at whatever petty grievance he had with his mother, he failed to notice Chloe following him. She scrambled up the rickety ladder, then laughed at his attempts to get her to come down. She didn't see the crack forming in the log beneath her legs. He begged her to listen, but she only laughed harder. Then the wood had cleaved apart, sending her tumbling to the ground.

He could still hear her scream.

You couldn't save her then, either.

"Oh, God," Elena whispered. She fell to her knees on the concrete beside Chloe's head and lifted the wet hair from her neck to reveal four lines of reddish-brown marks.

Until that moment, his mind had been fixed into the pattern of a tragic accident. Chloe had never been good with water. He'd tried to convince her to learn to swim so many times, but she'd always pushed it off. But when he saw the bruises, the truth of what had really happened bore down on him like a freight train. He slammed his closed fist down on the concrete, grunting as his skin split at the contact.

It wasn't an accident. Someone did this to her.

"What do we do?" Elena clasped her hands together. "We call someone. Right? We call the cops?"

Instead of answering, Sebastian retrieved his phone from his damp pants, grateful for the waterproof case, and dialed 911.

"Stillwood police station," a female voice answered. "How may I direct your call?"

He stared down at his little sister through a haze of unshed tears. He'd never see her walk down the aisle or hold a niece or nephew in his arms. His whole life had revolved around family. First as a young adult, taking care of his grief-stricken parents until they sickened and died. Then a seamless transition to watching out for his sister, gently guiding her through her college years. Even as an adult, she'd needed him. Only a few weeks earlier he'd had to undo the damage of a professional swindler who had wrapped her up in so many layers of fantasy she hadn't even realized how much of her savings she'd given away. He still had nightmares about that.

What am I going to do now?

Through the phone, there was a creak of a chair reclining. "Hello?"

"It's me, Sandra," he said, finally. "I need you to send someone up to the Cain house. It's Chloe. S-he," he cleared his throat. "There's been an incident."

He answered Sandra's litany of questions, then said goodbye and hit disconnect.

Elena touched his shoulder. "I'm so sorry."

He placed his hand over hers and squeezed. As strange as it was to be seeing her again after so long, her presence was soothing, like a balm on his scarred heart.

But what is she doing here? A suspicious part of his mind whispered.

He released her fingers and schooled his face into a stony mask before facing her. "Tell me you had nothing to do with this."

Her expression twisted in a look of abject horror. "How can you even ask that? She was like family to me."

He didn't stop to think if it was a good idea. He just said the first words that popped into his mind. "That didn't stop your mother."

She turned her back, and the sniffing that followed made him want to kick himself.

She's back for ten minutes, and already you're pushing her away.

"I'm sorry," he said. "I was out of line."

"It's fine," she replied. Then she crouched next to Chloe's body. "What do you think she was doing here?"

He sighed. "She loved this house. She said she could still feel Edward here."

His chest ached as he recalled his last conversation with his sister. Someone at the station had given her access to Edward's file. He'd begged her to let go of the past, and instead, she'd shoved autopsy photographs in his face. Things had been tense between them ever since.

You'll never get to apologize. She's dead, and it's all your fault.

Elena touched his arm, sympathy shining from her eyes. "Are you okay?"

He slammed the door on his emotions. "I'm fine."

The wail of a siren cut through the biting wind, making them both jump.

"That was fast," she said, and he mumbled his agreement. The station was miles away.

They walked around the side of the house as a patrol car barreled down the driveway, lights flashing, throwing up a cloud of dust. It screeched to a stop, and a uniformed officer stepped out. He spotted them and raised a hand in salute.

Sebastian copied the gesture, but Elena did not. She swayed back and forth, inches from the edge of the hill. That's when it hit him. It was too late to save his sister, but there was still someone he had to protect. He wrapped a hand around her elbow and ushered her back to the house. Once they were inside, she darted down a hallway, then returned with a heaping pile of towels, which she dropped in front of him.

He toweled himself mostly dry, then sat across from her at the small table. "Why didn't you tell me you were coming back?"

She turned her head toward the window. "I'm not staying. I'm just here to sell the house."

And sever the only thing left connecting her to Stillwood.

"Why?" he asked, even though he already knew the answer. "People have moved on. It's been a long time since—" Memories flashed back. Chloe screaming, sirens blaring, his parents sobbing on the couch.

She scowled. "You can say it. Since my mother killed your brother."

Silence fell between them until it was broken by the sound of splintering wood at the front of the house. He jogged to the front door and opened it.

Standing with his foot clean through a rotten board was the one person he had hoped not to see.

Why did it have to be Roth?

Watery gray eyes passed over Sebastian and focused over his shoulder. The man tugged free, stepped around Sebastian, and stuck out a hand.

"Ma'am. I'm Detective Roth. Stillwood Police Department."

Elena hesitated, then accepted the handshake. "Elena Cain."

Sebastian ground his molars together at the blatant dismissal. "Why did they send you?"

Roth shot him a dark look. "I was in the area. Dispatch said there's a body?"

Sebastian gestured to the door. "Near the pool. Come on."

Roth straightened his uniform, then followed them through the house and out the deck to the pool.

So, it began. What were they doing before finding the body? Had they seen anyone else? The questions were achingly familiar, drawing Sebastian back to the night the cops had questioned him at the station about his brother.

When he finished, Roth crouched down and peered at Chloe's neck.

"She was strangled, wasn't she?" Elena gulped. "Those bruises, they're finger marks."

"Might be," Roth said as he jotted down notes. "Wouldn't be the first." He flipped his notebook closed and stood. "I'm sorry for your loss, Mr. Castillo. Truly, I am. But I need you both to come with me to the station so we can record your statements."

"No!" Elena burst out. Then her cheeks reddened. "I mean, why? Can't you take our statements here?"

Roth shook his head. "Until the coroner determines the cause of death, I have to consider this a homicide."

Sebastian watched the rise and fall of Elena's chest. Was it something about cops? She looked like a rabbit staring down the end of a rifle.

"We can meet you at the station, Roth," Sebastian said. "I'm sure you have things to do here."

Roth scowled. "And have you leave town the minute I look away? I wasn't born yesterday, Castillo."

Elena clutched his arm and whispered in his ear, "Please, Bast. There's something about that man. I don't want to get in a car with him." Her eyes were so wide he could see the whites all the way around her pupils.

Is that what Chloe looked like at the end?

He imagined his sister looking into the face of the

man who had killed her. Had she begged for her life? Had she called out his name in the end?

Did you blame me for not being there for you, sister?

His heart ached at the thought, and he curled his arms protectively around Elena, pulled her into his chest, tucked her head into his shoulder. "I won't make you go with him," he murmured into his hair. He squeezed her tight and glared at the detective. "We wouldn't get five minutes out of town before someone reported us, Roth, and you know it. Don't make me call the sheriff."

Roth's glower darkened, but he nodded. "Fine. If you insist. I need to wait for the coroner, anyway. Go right to the station. I'll let them know you're coming."

Then Roth took out his radio and walked away.

"Thank you," Elena said, winding her arms around his back. She squeezed once before putting her palms on his chest and pressing lightly. He dropped his arms to his side, even as he longed to pull her close so he could breathe in the scent of her hair, feel her body snug against his.

"Ms. Cain!" Roth shouted.

Sebastian jerked his neck to the side. "What now?"

"She has to leave her car until it's been processed."

Elena looked crestfallen. "I see." She removed her keys from her pocket, but they slipped out of her shaking fingers and landed with a splat on the wet ground. Sebastian picked them up, shook off the mud, then handed them back.

"Don't worry about it," he said. "I'll drive."

Chapter 3

Elena clenched her hands beneath the wooden table separating her from Detective Roth in the small room. The white-washed concrete walls were bare except for a large mirror opposite a single door.

The detective stared at her, tapping his fingers on the table.

Tap, tap, tap, tap.

After they'd arrived at the station, the officers had hustled her inside the interrogation room, and Roth had entered soon after. He'd made her recite her version of events over and over until her voice had cracked, then had her write it all down while he watched in stony silence.

All of that she'd expected.

What had her on edge was the tattoo of a cobalt blue tarantula skittering up and down Roth's bare forearm.

"Here's why I am having trouble believing you, Ms. Cain," Roth said. "You're telling me you returned to Stillwood just in time to find a dead body in your pool?"

Tap, tap, tap, tap.

She swallowed a knot in her throat.

"I—"

The spider raised its legs in a threatening posture. Roth leaned forward.

"Don't lie."

Tap, tap, tap, tap.

"I'm not—"

"I can tell when you're lying," Roth said. "I would advise you to tell the truth."

Tap, tap—

She slammed her hand on top of his. "Please! Stop doing that."

Roth grasped her fingers, jerking her forward. "Are you and Castillo in this together? Was it your idea or his?"

"What?"

The sudden intensity in his voice startled her. She tugged her arm, but he'd trapped her fingers in his steely grip.

He grinned, a predator waiting to strike. "Admit it. You killed her."

"I didn't kill her!"

The tarantula crawled across their joined hands, making her skin prickle. Its simmering anger pressed against her mind like a knife piercing her skull.

A wave of nausea rocked through her, and she vomited up what little food she'd eaten since last her captor had visited. The small room she was trapped in had no clock or windows, so it was impossible to tell how much time had passed. She ticked away the days by scratching lines on the cement walls with a small piece of chalk.

She rolled over and pressed her heated skin against the cool floor. Hunger was her constant companion, digging its claws into her stomach. But she had hope—a twisted piece of spring that she'd broken off the bed frame.

The next time the man came to see her, she'd use it to take away his weapons.

Both of them.

The memory ended abruptly, but residual fear thrummed through her like the reverberations of a plucked string. Then, remembering her self-defense classes—better late than never—she relaxed her arm. Roth's hold loosened, and she used the chance to slip her hand away, then tucked it beneath the table.

The tarantula prowled her skin, probing her mind for weakness.

"For the fifth time," she said, enunciating each word. "I came back to sell the house. Chloe was dead when I arrived."

"Really?" Roth's voice dripped with skepticism. He sat back in his chair. "I guess I shouldn't be surprised. Murder runs in your family, doesn't it?"

She clenched her hands into fists, her fingernails cutting into her palms, and imagined reaching out, grabbing Roth around the neck, strangling the life out of him. It would be so easy. All she had to do was let the tarantula take over.

No.

The thoughts, fantasies, swirling around her mind weren't her own. It was the shade, searching for leverage. She could feel its hatred of Roth, its desire to hurt him.

What does that mean?

With the detective still staring at her, a shit-eating-grin on his face, she worked up her simmering anger into a furious rage. Then she sent out a mental blast with all the emotion she could muster.

The shade reappeared on Roth's hands. Its legs curled inwards as if she had sprayed it with pesticide.

It worked!

The unexpected victory filled her with a bubbling sense of accomplishment, and she tried to remember something from the police procedurals she'd watched as a kid that would convince Roth to back off. When it finally came to her, it was so obvious that she wanted to kick herself.

"Why am I even sitting here?" she hated the warble in her voice. "I don't have to talk to you. I want my lawyer."

David would be furious, but she trusted him to get her out of the mess she'd landed herself in.

The detective pushed back his chair with a metallic screech that made her cringe. "We'll get right on that."

After he exited, a band of iron closed around her chest. When Roth had brought her into the room, it hadn't seemed so bad.

The door slammed shut.

Her heart pounded in her ears. The room was so small. There wasn't enough air. She would suffocate, and they'd find her body, limp and pale like Chloe.

She flattened her hands on the table. Soon she'd be hyperventilating, and wouldn't that be perfect?

The suspect went into a panic attack in the interrogation room; she imagined the prosecutor saying. *Her guilty conscience couldn't take it.*

The lights flickered with a crackling sound, but she was only dimly aware of it. She squeezed her eyes shut and thought of wide-open spaces, fields full of flowers, and anything else that wasn't the small, dark room shrinking around her.

"Psst, hey!"

Elena jumped, making the chair beneath her rattle. A woman stared at her from the open door. There was a shade on her flushed cheek, a miniature seal-point Persian cat. It opened its mouth in a silent yawn and curled into a ball, tucking its face under its fluffy tail.

"What are you waiting for?" The woman asked. "Come out of there!"

The woman lunged inside and grasped her wrist. As their skin touched, a thin current of static electricity arced between them. Then the woman dragged her into the hallway. Free of the confined space, the band around Elena's chest dissolved, and she took great gulps of air like a drowning victim freed from the surf.

"Thank you," she said, leaning her back against the cool wall. Her savior, a plump woman with curly brown hair and sparkling eyes, closed the door to the interrogation room. She wore faded overalls and a thick leather belt around her waist, filled with tools. She smiled, and the expression transformed her face from ordinary to striking—handsome, if not pretty.

The Persian fluffed its tail and scampered away.

Elena tensed, expecting the shade to assault her the way the tarantula had, but nothing happened.

"Sorry for barging in," the woman said. "I saw you through the glass, and I could tell you were about to have a straight-up panic attack. I'd say it's nice to meet you, but I suspect you've had better days. Hi, I'm Sandra."

The woman stuck out a hand, and Elena cautiously took it. When there was no electric discharge, she relaxed. "You could say that again. My legs feel like spaghetti. I'm—"

Sandra pumped her hand up and down. "I know who you are. Everyone here knows you."

"Ah. I guess I should have expected that. What are you doing back here?"

Sandra kicked the interrogation room door with her foot and rattled the door handle. "Lock sticks." She grabbed a screwdriver from her belt and, with an efficiency Elena admired, popped the handle from the door and fitted it with a new one. "That'll do it."

"Thanks again," Elena said. "I don't want to think about what would have happened if you hadn't let me out of there. I'm not good with small spaces."

"I believe you," Sandra said. She hoisted her tool bag onto her shoulder. "I'm the same with spiders. One time, when I was a kid, I was doing my paper route, and I had just got to McPherson's house when I looked down, and this huge spider had crawled around from the other side of the bike handle onto the back of my hand. I haven't ridden a bike since, not without checking the handles. Come on, follow me. I'll show you out. I work dispatch on weekends, so I know my way around."

Elena struggled to follow the rapid conversation. "Won't you get in trouble for letting me out?"

"It's fine. When Roth barged out, I heard the sheriff tell him to release you. Roth's just being an ass."

It wasn't the first time Elena had made an enemy, but what had she done to deserve such treatment?

"What's his problem, anyway?" She fisted her right hand and knocked it against the wall as they walked. Her mother had called it "waking the spirits." Elena called it a bad habit, one that required her to wash her hands more often than necessary.

Sandra clicked her tongue. "Rumor was Roth and Chloe had a thing back in the day. And it's not like Stillwood gets a lot of action for a rookie cop. This is only the second murder in—" Sandra bit her lip. "Sorry, me and my big mouth."

Elena waved it off. "It's fine. If I'm going to be here for more than a few days, I'm going to have to get used to it."

Since my original plans have been blown out of the water.

She hadn't driven far—Stillwood was only a few hundred miles away from her apartment—but it would have to be far enough. With luck, the Harvester would find a new target, and she would have some time before having to deal with it again.

"That's the problem with living in a small town," Sandra said softly. "People don't forget."

They rounded another corner. Elena glanced down the hallway, then spun around. Wasn't the entrance in the opposite direction? "Uh, hey, not that I don't appreciate letting me out, but where are we going?"

Sandra adjusted her tool belt higher on her hips. "Evidence."

"Oh, no, they left my things at the front desk."

"I know."

Sandra turned and continued walking. Unsure of what to do, Elena followed. At the end of the hall, Sandra kneeled and removed a black tube from her pocket. She popped the silver lid with her thumb and carefully withdrew a roll of film.

"Calm down," Sandra said before Elena could ask what she was doing, "I can feel your anxiety all over my back. We'll be out of here in a minute. I just have to pick something up first."

She pushed the loop of film through the top of the door, inch by inch. When a few feet remained, she slid it over until it was directly above the handle and tugged.

The door clicked and swung open. Only then did she

realize that Sandra had caught the handle from the other side.

"How'd you learn how to do that?"

Sandra slid the film back into the tube and gave a toothy smile. "Don't ask questions you don't want to know the answers to. Now sit tight and watch the hall. If you see anyone coming, tell them you got lost. I don't know. You'll think of something."

Elena took a hasty step back. "Woah, woah, I'm not doing this."

"Wanna go back in the box? One shout, and my dad will come running."

"Your dad?"

"The sheriff."

Elena braced an arm on the wall. "Your father is the sheriff, and you're breaking into the evidence room?"

"Yep. And don't think you can run off on your own. It's a maze in here. You'd get lost for sure."

Elena searched the ceiling for cameras. Uniformed officers might come around the corner at any moment. The longer they remained, the more likely that vision was to come to pass. She made a shooting motion with her hands. "Okay. Fine. Finish whatever it is you're here to do, and let's get out of here."

Sandra entered the room. Elena turned and kept her gaze focused on the hall, straining to see both directions at once.

"Wait, is that why you let me out? To be your spotter?"

"Worked, didn't it?"

Elena groaned. "Hurry up, will you?"

Sandra popped back out of the room, holding a laptop under her arm. "Got it. Let's fly." She darted away, faster than seemed possible for her size, and Elena was forced to follow through the winding maze of corridors. At every turn, she expected to see a barrage of police officers waiting for them, but they made it to the lobby without incident.

Elena took a deep breath just as a strong hand grasped her shoulder. Sandra's face loomed close. "Be careful," she said. "They are watching."

Alarms blared in Elena's head. "Who is watching? What does that mean?"

Sandra winked. "It means I'm on your side." She turned and strolled out of the station, leaving Elena with far more questions than she'd had before.

Chapter 4

Sebastian tapped his heels against the floor. Not because he was irritated or impatient, but because it made the detective sitting across from him in the tiny room squirm.

"You know, despite what you think," Roth said, a muscle in his jaw twitching. "You weren't the only one who cared about her. We're on the same side, Castillo."

The sympathy in those words were like a punch to the gut. He remembered Chloe's face, her unblinking eyes, the bruises on her throat.

It's your fault she's dead.

The pain in his heart festered into anger, and he let it billow up and consume him.

"That's pathetic, even for you, Roth," he said with a sneer. "Have you ever even seen an interrogation? You have to lay out a scenario, get me to admit to something. What kind of detective are you?"

He knew the words were cruel, but he couldn't help the pain from escaping.

The muscle in Roth's jaw twitched again. "This isn't the movies, Mr. Castillo."

Sebastian shrugged. "You have my statement. What do you think I am lying about?"

"Where were you on..." Roth shuffled his papers around. One sheet slid off the edge of the table and fluttered to the floor. Roth grabbed for it, but Sebastian snagged it with the toe of his boot and dragged it across the floor, out of the detective's reach.

"Wow, look at that," Sebastian said. It was the statement he'd written up an hour earlier. "I thought you'd have shredded it by now."

Roth thumped back in his chair. "Those are very serious allegations, Mr. Castillo."

Sebastian slid the sheet across the table toward the detective. "That's what you keep saying."

The detective leaned forward. "You sure you didn't just get mad at Chloe and push her? I've seen how violent you can get when you're angry."

Sebastian's cheeks heated. "That only happened once. And it was an accident. She was my sister, God dammit. I'd never do anything to hurt her."

A few weeks prior, Roth had caught him and Chloe in an argument. His sister had insisted upon borrowing his car when he wasn't home, leading him to suspect it was stolen. When he finally figured it out, he called off the cops, but not before Chloe gave him one of her signature shoulder punches, and Sebastian responded in kind. It had been an innocent exchange, but Roth had arrived just in time to see it and assume the worst.

If he's already got his mind set against me, there's nothing I can do.

"I'm not saying another word until I talk to a lawyer," Sebastian said.

That shut Roth up fast, and he stormed out of the room, letting the door slam behind him.

As Sebastian waited, staring at the large mirror across from him, he wondered if Elena was doing okay. Anxiety had been radiating off her in waves when they'd arrived at the station. He'd had to pry her fingers off his arm when all he wanted to do was throw his arms around her.

She's an adult now. She can take care of herself.

He kept looking for the girl he'd known but couldn't find her. The bright smiles and laughter were nowhere to be seen. It was as if she'd holed herself up so no one else could touch her.

The door creaked open, and an officer stepped inside, indicating with a hand wave that he was free to leave. The officer guided him out into the lobby, where Elena was waiting.

She stood next to Roth by the intake desk, her chin lowered, her gaze fixed on Roth's crossed arms, like a child being scolded. Her eyes flicked back and forth as if scanning the words on a page.

He approached from behind Roth and mouthed the words *are you okay?*

She offered a slight nod and turned her attention back to Roth. The detective turned and frowned. "Sheriff says I have to let you go." His glower could've soured milk. "Don't leave town."

"You know, it's been a long day," Elena said. "I'm exhausted. If we're free to go, I think we should be leaving." She hooked an arm through Sebastian's and dragged him away from Roth, who was still glaring daggers.

Once they were outside, her hair lifted in the wind, flying behind her like a banner. She gathered it together with practiced ease and twisted it into a knot at the back of her neck.

"You should leave it loose," he said, brushing the back of his hand along the side of her head. Her long, flowing hair had always appealed to him. He imagined it draped around him, the silky length sliding against his skin.

"Too much trouble," she replied. But a flush graced her neck and cheekbones. The color suited her, a pale rose that gave her otherwise translucent skin a cozy glow.

What am I thinking?

He forced his wayward thoughts back on track and checked his watch. "It's late. We should get some food before the supper rush."

Elena nodded. "I'm hungry. Although I don't know how I can be."

"Runty's changed ownership a few years ago," he said. "But it's more or less the same place. Hop in. My treat."

He unlocked the door, and they climbed inside.

They drove for a while in awkward silence, punctuated only by the sound of wind roaring around the car and the occasional thump of tires.

Elena squeezed her arms around her chest and leaned her head against the window. Then he hit a rut in the road, and she yelped. He grasped her shoulder.

"You okay?"

She twisted away, crowding the passenger door as if his touch had scalded her. He put his hand back on the wheel and tried not to show how much her withdrawal had hurt him. What had she been through that had made her so skittish? The girl he'd known had never shied away from his embrace.

She's not yours to protect, his brain reminded him. *No matter how much you want to.*

But focusing on Elena kept him from thinking about his sister and the pain she had to have experienced. Were his parents looking down on him from heaven, ashamed he hadn't saved her?

His eyes started to burn, and he forced the thoughts away. He could cry later.

He turned off the main road and into a strip mall parking lot, then turned off the car. He reached for the door, but Elena stopped him with a hand on his other arm.

"Give me a minute," she said. There was a slight tremor in her voice. She covered her face with her hands. "Sorry. I just..." her words were thick and slurred. "I keep thinking about how Chloe will never sit in a restaurant again. She'll never go for a coffee, have a stroll outside. She's gone, and I never got to tell her so many things." Her eyes glittered with tears. "Did she hate me? Did she blame me for what happened to Edward? I don't know how to do this."

Her distress resonated with him, and he had to swallow heavily before he could speak without tearing up himself. Instead, he put an arm around her. This time she didn't pull back but leaned into him. He touched his nose to her hair. She smelled like soap with a faint hint of roses.

"For me, it lasted weeks, maybe months," he said, remembering his brother's death. "I got angry. Then depressed. I reconsidered every decision I made, trying to find the one choice that might have led to a different ending." He closed his eyes, fighting tears. "It's a pointless search. But you won't understand that until you've chased down every possibility. Eventually, you'll come to realize the decisions you made are long gone." He squeezed her. "It can be difficult reconciling the truth with your version of reality, but you will cope."

He curled his fingers around her other arm and hissed when he touched her skin.

"You're frozen!" He snagged his jacket from the back seat and draped it around her shoulders. Then he popped open the glove compartment, took out a pair of leather gloves, and placed them on her lap. "I think you need these more than me."

She picked up the gloves with a smile, then looked at him, and the smile wiped off her face. She stared at his neck and murmured something beneath her breath.

He splayed his fingers around his throat, expecting to feel a smudge of dirt or leaf. "What? Is there something on my neck?"

"No. Nothing." She jerked her head away. "I'm hungry. Let's go in."

****

"You weren't kidding," Elena said, holding the door open for Sebastian. The bell above the diner door chimed. "It looks exactly the same."

The floor was tiled in a black and white checkerboard pattern. Framed photographs lined the wood-paneled walls above padded leather booths. Nestled in the center of each was a plastic tray holding glass containers of sugar, salt, ketchup, and vinegar. Not white vinegar, but balsamic, the kind Chloe had loved to drench her fries in even after they teased her of pickling her tongue.

Elena's chest ached as she remembered Chloe laughing maniacally as she dispensed the dark liquid over her fries. There was too much Chloe in Stillwood. Everywhere she looked brought back a memory.

And the killer was still out there, possibly planning his next move.

I won't let him get away with it.

There was the little matter of the Harvester, but it wasn't as if she had the money to leave. Somehow, she doubted the police would let her sell the house while it was an active crime scene.

"Look at that," Sebastian said. "Someone's doing the challenge." He nodded to a crowd surrounding a table in the corner. "Chloe wants to try it on the long weekend." He blinked. "I mean, she was going to."

The crumpled look on his face, like a lost child in a department store surrounded by strangers, stirred Elena's heart, and she threaded her fingers with his. "Let's go check it out."

They crossed the restaurant and joined the back of the crowd.

"Pe-ter! Pe-ter!" A man chanted. "You got this!"

They maneuvered through the onlookers to see a man sitting at a table behind the largest hamburger Elena had ever seen. His white dress shirt was stained with flecks of grease, and his striped, blue tie was flung over his shoulder. He shoveled fistfuls of fries into his mouth with both hands, pausing only to chug water from one of the many glasses on the table.

"I don't know if he's falling apart or what," Sebastian said.

She leaned closer so he could hear him over the noise. "You know this guy?"

Sebastian grimaced. "Unfortunately."

Ding.

The bell above the door chimed, and a woman stormed inside. She wore a sleek black dress that hugged her slim figure and shiny black heels.

"You're in trouble now, Peter," Sebastian said.

The woman spotted them and walked over. Her gaze passed over Elena as if she was invisible and landed on Sebastian. "Have you seen my husband?"

Sebastian shook his head. "Try the hospital?"

Elena glanced back at the table, but it was empty. The rear door to the restaurant, a few feet away, banged against the outside of the building in the wind.

Sebastian was talking. She wrenched her attention back to him. "Sorry, what?"

"I said, let's get a table."

After they found a seat and Sebastian was tearing the paper wrapper around his bundle of cutlery, Elena felt compelled to comment. "I'm impressed you lied with such a straight face."

Sebastian snorted. "I don't know if Janet counts. They have one of the most dysfunctional relationships I've ever seen. You know, she lost her job for stealing products. From a boutique store, where they count inventory three times a day. Of course, Peter found out, and—"

A server appeared at their table, clutching three laminated menus in one wrinkled hand. Elena accepted one and hissed in a breath. The woman's eyes were black from corner to corner, and her lips were spread, revealing a mouthful of sharpened teeth.

"You thought you could run, did you?" The creature rasped. "I'll always find you. Haven't you figured that out yet?"

Sebastian put down his menu and touched her wrist. "What's wrong?"

This can't be happening.

The server pulled a battered pad of paper from her pocket. "You folks ready to order?" Her voice was smokers' rough, her teeth yellowed and square. Her eyes weren't black at all but dark brown.

You're losing it.

Elena pressed her hands flat to the worn tabletop. She'd been through a traumatic event and was imagining things. That's all.

She glanced at the menu and handed it back. "I'll take a sunshine breakfast, please. White toast, bacon, and *hard* scrambled eggs."

It was closer to supper, but breakfast was her comfort food, and she desperately needed comfort.

After a moment of silence, Sebastian also handed his menu back. "Black coffee."

The server flipped over a coffee cup, filled it, then limped away. Sebastian propped his elbows on the table. "You want to tell me what that was about?"

Elena copied his pose, putting her chin on the backs of her hands. "It was nothing. I thought I recognized her, but I was wrong."

Her heart still thrummed in her chest, but the shock of seeing those black eyes was fading.

God knows I've had a stressful day. That must be it, my imagination going wild.

The Harvester couldn't have found her so quickly. Not again.

Sebastian tapped a finger on the table a few times, then shrugged. "If you say so." He sipped his coffee. "So, what did Roth ask you?"

Elena scowled. "He thinks we're involved."

The questions Roth had shot at her would've boiled her blood if she hadn't been so surprised by the shade he carried.

A shade that, for whatever reason, harbored a deep

rage for Roth. Was it because Roth was the killer she had seen in the woman's memory? That was a chilling thought. But she couldn't bring that up to Sebastian. "What do you think Chloe was doing at the house?"

Sebastian's face crumpled. "She left a note on my car, asking to meet." He rubbed his face. "She was always doing that. I kept telling her just text me, but you know what she was like."

"It's not your fault," Elena said. Then she snorted. "Listen to me. I'm telling you exactly what I didn't want to hear."

Sebastian smiled. "I appreciate it, anyway."

She met his eyes and saw a reflection of her own pain.

I missed you. I missed you so much it hurt.

She'd tried dating other men, but they were always too short, too mean-tempered, too blonde, too severe, too cold. The truth she'd been too blind to see was now obvious. Their only real flaw was not being Sebastian.

She curled her fingers around his, but before she could say anything more, the server returned with their food, and Elena yanked her hand away.

Sebastian's expression smoothed into a cool mask.

This is for the best.

Keeping him at a distance hurt, but they were both grieving. A romance would only complicate things, and he deserved better than the daughter of the woman who had murdered his brother.

She turned her attention to her food, pouring a generous dollop of ketchup on her hash browns, which made them decently palatable. Nothing could save the eggs.

Sebastian sipped his coffee. "Not what you

wanted?"

She shot him a dirty look. "I hate wet eggs."

"You could send them back."

"And draw even more attention to myself? No thanks."

But she was hungry enough to clear most of her plate with only a small amount of grumbling.

"So, what's with Roth?" she asked when she finished. "Why does he hate you?"

Sebastian set his mug down hard. "It's a long story."

"I have time." She toyed with the piece of paper wrapped around her cutlery. She'd always found it easier to talk to people when her hands were occupied. She folded the paper into a miniature fortune teller and then a crane.

Sebastian tapped his fingers on the table.

She flicked the crane toward him. "Please don't do that."

He curled his fingers. "Sorry. It was a few years ago. He was a cadet, then. He showed up at my office one night. He wanted my permission to date Chloe."

Elena snorted. "What? Talk about old-fashioned."

Sebastian took another sip of coffee. "I thought it was respectful. They went out on three dates before she dumped him. But Roth wouldn't let it go. He showed up at the house, called all hours of the night."

"What did you do?"

"I reported him to the department."

"And?"

"What do you think happened? With my record?"

She could see it in her head, the cops weighing the word of a troubled young man against that of a respected member of the force.

"It didn't matter that Roth was only a cadet. He was part of the team." Sebastian's hands clenched around the coffee cup, the tips of his fingers turning white. "Evidence collected at the hospital disappeared. Witnesses who had seen Roth push Chloe around refused to talk. That was the last straw. I threatened to go to the press. Two weeks later, Roth transferred to Minneapolis. Problem solved. But the bastard couldn't cut it in the city. He was back within a year. I was prepared to confront him, but he kept his distance from Chloe, so I left him alone."

"I see," Elena said. She imagined Sebastian knocking Roth out. No wonder he had come after them with such vigor.

Then she spotted movement on Sebastian's shoulders. The snake was back, winding its way around his neck and up to his jawline.

A tingling started in her fingers.

Don't even try it.

She shored up her mental defenses and tried not to let her emotions show while pushing at the shade in her mind. It wasn't enough.

He was so cold that he could no longer feel it. His thighs pulsed with a dull warmth, and the occasional sharp pain radiated up his arm.

There was a plastic mask on his face. He tried to move his hands, but they remained stubbornly by his side, weighed down by something soft and heavy. His legs were equally paralyzed.

He had to get out. There was someone he needed to see. It was very important he talk to this person, warn them of what had happened. But then the name and face of the person flitted out of his mind like a piece of lint on the wind.

He cried out, a plaintive sound that bounced around the room.

"What?" Sebastian clutched at his shirt. "Did I spill?"

The snake had returned to its position on his neck, its head facing away from her. From the memory, she knew the shade had come from a man who had suffered when he'd been alive. Why had it imprinted upon Sebastian?

It doesn't matter.

The shade didn't deserve her sympathy. Whatever tragedy it had gone through wasn't her problem. She had enough of a mess to deal with.

Elena shook her head. "It's nothing."

"So, what's next? You can't go back to the house. Roth will have it all taped up."

Elena shrugged. "Get a hotel, probably."

She wanted to get back in her car and high tail it out of town before the Harvester caught up with her, but that would be the quickest way to turn her into suspect number one. She would just have to keep a close eye on the people around her and be ready to run at a moment's notice.

In other words, nothing new.

"You could stay with me," Sebastian said, with an upward inflection that didn't quite make it a question.

It was a generous offer. One she should've jumped at, given the lean state of her bank account.

And it would give you a chance to pursue the heat simmering between you.

That was the most tempting part of all, the opportunity for a human connection, if only for a short time.

"I know it's probably weird," Sebastian said. "But I've got plenty of space, and to be honest," he slid the index finger of his left hand around the rim of his coffee cup. "I'd rather not be alone right now."

You'd be putting him in danger. He's not safe around you. No one is. You could kill him as easily as your mother killed his brother.

The image of her mother holding a bloody knife flashed in her mind.

"I'm sorry," she said, avoiding his gaze. "I don't think that would be a good idea."

His face froze over again. He took out his wallet, thumbed through the bills with jerking motions, and then placed a handful on the table.

"It's not you, really," she said, desperate for him to understand.

"Don't," he said, holding up a hand. "You're right. It's better this way."

As the server returned with the bill and then counted out Sebastian's change, his words echoed in her mind.

It's better this way.

Chapter 5

The atmosphere in the car was tense. Elena kept her hands clasped together between her legs as the trees blurred past the passenger window. The radio cut in and out between bursts of static until she tired of the sound and turned the volume all the way down.

The car hit a pothole, and she bounced in her seat. She stared at the horizon and breathed through her mouth until her stomach settled. "Okay, I get it. You're mad. Don't take it out on my stomach."

Sebastian's hands clenched on the wheel, but he muttered an apology and slowed down.

After leaving the diner, he had taken her back to the house, where she'd begged the officers at the scene to let her access her car so she could grab her luggage. Although they had been initially cautious of letting her past the yellow crime scene tape, they had eventually relented.

Thank God for that.

She didn't want to think about how meager her savings were without having to buy all new clothes and toiletries.

But things had only gotten worse when they were back in the car, and Sebastian had calmly listed all the reasons she should stay with him.

There's still a killer out there. It's safer to stay together. You'd save the cost of a motel.

As much as her heart ached to refuse him, that's exactly what she did. He couldn't understand the danger he was putting himself in by staying around her, and since she couldn't explain, she was left with no other choice.

She turned her head and spotted a splotch of emerald ink on his neck. Her words dissolved; gaze locked on the spot. But no memory came, and the python slithered around Sebastian's neck and disappeared under his shirt. Relieved, she returned her attention to their surroundings.

They passed a lit sign that switched between the words Motel and Hotel in red neon. Some of the letters were burned out, advertising the Hamilton Arms as a '*lotel*' with '*free wif.*'

It was, unfortunately, the best she could afford.

Sebastian maneuvered around a large pothole in the parking lot to stop outside the glass-enclosed reception area. The windows were splattered with mud, and an ice machine whined away in the corner, one of its silver doors propped open.

"It's even more run down than I remember," Sebastian said. He flicked his gaze at her. "Are you seriously going to stay here?"

Instead of answering, Elena exited the car. Sebastian followed and stood behind her as she handed over three of the precious bills remaining in her wallet to a young man with a sleeping owl on his cheek.

She signed her name and accepted a tarnished copper key attached to a block of wood with the muttered "*up the stairs to the right.*"

Once they were outside, it started raining. A drizzle at first, but soon fat drops pounded the sidewalk and formed rivers that washed cigarette butts into the gutters.

She ascended the stairs, Sebastian in close pursuit. When they reached the door matching the number on the key, she spun around. "Enough! Why are you still here?"

He blinked.

She crossed her arms.

He stuck out his lower lip and widened his eyes like a kicked puppy. It was the same look he'd used to convince her to sneak out and go skinny dipping one cold summer night. He knew she couldn't resist that look.

He was right.

"Fine. Okay!" She threw up her arms. "You can stay, but only for a few hours."

His jaw relaxed, and he brushed her hand with his, taking her bag and hefting it on his shoulder. The brief contact sent a jolt of electricity up her arm and caused butterflies to erupt in her stomach.

She fumbled the key into the lock and turned it until the latch clicked.

"Let me go first," Sebastian said.

She shrugged and stepped away. He stepped inside, then held the door for her to pass. She flicked on the light, took a deep breath, then gagged. The room smelled musty and sour, like the inside of a fridge that hadn't been cleaned for months. The thin brown carpet was worn through in places, and the dresser across from the twin bed was missing two drawers on the bottom.

The door slammed behind her, and then something hit it from the other side.

Thump

Elena backed into the room, her mind filled with images of sharpened teeth and cackling laughter.

Thump

The Harvester had found her, and once it possessed her body and consumed her soul, it would ravage Sebastian the way it had slaughtered Edward when it had possessed her mother.

The oppressive crush she'd been living with for over a decade returned with a vengeance. Would she ever be free, or would she continue running for the rest of her life?

Sebastian walked past her and opened the door a crack, just enough to see outside. He murmured something, then closed the door again.

"Who was it?" her was voice high and tight. She cleared her throat self-consciously.

"Housekeeping. They asked if we needed more towels."

The tension rushed from her body like a pricked balloon. "Oh."

He put his hands on her shoulders. "Are you sure you're okay?"

"I'm fine," she lied.

Hands clasped like iron bands around her neck and pushed her face-first into the pool.

Chloe had suffered so much. What if it was the Harvester, after all? What if it had taken Chloe to get to her? Did that make her a murderer?

Maybe this is my fault, after all.

"You don't look fine," Sebastian said. He slid his arms down her back and tugged her closer. She let him, turning her head and resting it on his chest. He was so warm. She wished she could bury herself in the heat coming off his body. She slipped her hands beneath his shirt, running her fingertips over the muscles of his back.

"Scratch," he murmured.

She dug her nails in and drew them down, eliciting a long sigh.

"I always thought it was weird that you liked that," she said, rubbing over the place she'd scratched. Then her hands drifted lower, grazing the waistband of his jeans.

Her stomach growled.

Sebastian burst into wheezing laughter. "W-what? How can you be hungry? We just ate!"

Elena's cheeks warmed, and she turned away. "I wouldn't call that food."

The paltry breakfast had barely filled her up, and she had no intention of telling Sebastian how slim her grocery bill had been over the past month.

They made their way to the fast-food restaurant across the street, then carried the greasy paper bags back to the room. Elena refused to apologize for the mountain of food she'd ordered, despite the jokes he cracked at her expense.

"Should I go back and buy more?" he popped a fry into his mouth.

She scowled and wiped crumbs from her face with a sleeve.

He muttered an apology and slid his untouched hamburger forward.

She took it and peeled the burger from its foil wrapper. Her mouth watered at the savory smell of bacon and caramelized onions combined with the acidic tang of mustard.

"Your appetite hasn't changed," he said. "I remember we used to laugh at how you ate twice as much as anyone else. What was it Chloe called you?"

She grunted. "Sorry. Don't remember."

"Lucky for you, I do, Ella Leftovers."

She groaned. "It wasn't my fault. Remember what my mother put in my school lunches? What kind of woman sends her teenage daughter to school with fermented herring and cottage cheese?"

"It stunk up the whole cafeteria," Sebastian said. Then he laughed so hard his shoulders shook. He waved a hand. "Sorry, I know. Not funny."

She sniffed. "Well, it was a little funny." She crumpled the burger's foil wrapper and added it to the growing pile of garbage on the table. Then she looked out the window, where the sky was stained red and orange. How had the time passed so quickly?

"You should go," she said, flicking a ball of foil off the table.

Sebastian took her hand. "What if I don't want to?"

The droning sound of the ice maker faded into the background. He rubbed his thumb along her palm. Her eyes fluttered closed. His fingers touched her cheek, and she leaned into his touch.

"Lay with me."

She staggered back. "What?

The grip on her fingers tightened. "Not like that. Like when we were kids, watching the clouds."

It was a bad idea. A really bad idea. But some part of her yearned for comfort, for his touch. She'd denied herself for so long. What was one night, in the grand scheme of things? Just one night, after more than a decade of longing.

They lay on the bed together, Elena's head on his shoulder. She listened to his steady heartbeat, breathed in the smell of his menthol aftershave. She threw an arm across his chest and squirmed closer. "Tell me about

Chloe. About the woman she grew into."

Sebastian sighed, and his breath tickled her forehead. "She wanted out of here. More than anything. She flitted from one thing to the next, never keeping with a passion long enough to make a living. A few years ago, she told me she'd become a painter. She closed herself up for weeks at a time, churning out dozens of paintings. I still have a few of them. She had genuine talent. But, like everything else, she tired of it and stopped."

"She was a dreamer," Elena said. "I miss her."

Sebastian squeezed his arm around her waist "She missed you, too. She talked about you all the time."

She lifted her head. "Oh?"

"Yeah." He bumped the tip of his nose against hers. "But I missed you more."

The next thing she knew, his lips were pressed against hers, and her insides were melting.

He tasted salty, of fries and grease, and his body was warm against her. She clung tighter, wishing he could envelop her completely and hide her away from the creatures hunting her. She met his mouth with her own, tangling her tongue with his. Heat curled through her belly, down to her toes.

"Touch me," she said. Her breasts were swollen and heavy, and the slight friction of her shirt against her nipples was agonizing.

He cupped her breast, rubbing a thumb over her erect nipple.

The sound of a door slamming jerked her back into the present.

What am I doing?

Getting involved with him would invite heartbreak. She slid off him and busied herself with emptying her backpack onto the bed. Anything to occupy her hands.

"I'm sorry," Sebastian said in a husky voice that made her insides squirm.

She muttered something unintelligible, unable to find the words to express how he made her feel. Long gone was the boy she'd shared clumsy kisses with. They'd both changed. And yet, the dull throbbing in her pelvis suggested the spark between them was alive and well.

Don't get attached. Remember the plan. Once Chloe's murder is solved, it'll be time to get out of town.

She upended her bag onto the mattress and dug through her possessions, throwing clothing left and right.

Sebastian touched her shoulder. "What's wrong?"

"I'm not sure." She paused, then spotted it. An object, sitting at the edge of the pile, a black canvas sack no bigger than her palm. "Shit. Someone's been through my stuff."

"How do you know?"

Her pulse pounded in her ears. She pointed to the sack with a shaking finger. "That's not mine."

Sebastian palmed the unknown item and slid the zipper open along the edge. A metallic smell filled the room, causing a shudder to rip through her.

She crowded closer. "Let me see."

He lifted the sack out of her reach. "You don't want to see this."

She folded her arms over her chest. "I'm not a little girl, Bast."

He sighed and handed it over.

She peered inside to see a pair of swimming goggles caked in blood. Written on the lenses in black ink were the words *get out*.

"W-what do you think it means?" she asked.

Was it Chloe's killer telling her to leave town?

Sebastian snapped the container shut and let the goggles fall to the bed. "Pack your things. We're leaving."

"For once, I agree with you," Elena said, already ramming her possessions back into her bag until the only thing left was the goggles. She grimaced, then picked them up and shoved them into a separate zippered compartment. "Where are we going?"

Sebastian slipped her bag out of her fingers, onto his shoulder, and held the door open.

"Where I should have taken you to begin with. Home."

Chapter 6

Elena usually had no problem sleeping in unfamiliar beds. Years of living a nomadic lifestyle, where comfort and familiarity bred danger, had trained her body to fall asleep the moment her head hit the pillow. But as she lay on the narrow daybed in Sebastian's guest room slash office and stared at the ceiling, sleep refused to come.

She couldn't stop thinking about the goggles in her bag, about what they meant. Someone obviously wanted her out of town, but who? And why?

Then she remembered Chloe's last memory; the large hands wrapped around her neck, the burn of water filling her lungs. Something in that memory bothered her, a sense of despair caused by more than the assault.

She knew him.

That was the unpleasant fact she'd been dancing around all day. Chloe had known her murderer, had trusted him.

What did that mean?

She lifted the blanket from her chest and looked at the yellow boa resting above her breasts. "It would help if you could tell me who he is." The shade curled into a tighter ball, tucking its head beneath its body.

So much for that.

She tossed and turned. Had she met the murderer? Walked right past him, talked to him, without knowing?

In the end, it wasn't anxiety or insomnia that got her

out of bed but the rumbling in her stomach. She kicked off the heavy blankets and stepped into the hallway, her cold toes numb on the wood floor, one hand trailing along the wall. The headlights of the cars driving past the building shone through the windows and cast her shadow behind her in bursts of light.

She tiptoed down the hall, then stopped when she smelled something odd.

Freshly baked bread?

She peeked into the kitchen to see Sebastian crouched in front of the oven. He wore a pink, flower-print apron around his waist, oven mitts, and nothing else.

Wow.

His wide shoulders were dusted with curly dark hairs and graced by the same green tree python. It slithered around to look at her, then flicked its tongue and returned to its previous position.

She lowered her gaze to the apron strings tied around Sebastian's narrow waist and then lower to the firm globes of his rear. Only then did she remember her manners and clear her throat. "Hey."

Sebastian peeked over his shoulder. "Hey." His gaze fell, and his mouth dropped open.

That's when she realized her mistake—she was as naked as he.

"Oh God!"

She covered her breasts with her hands and backpedaled into the hallway, and then ran to the guest bedroom. She shrugged on her clothes before making her way back to the kitchen to find Sebastian sitting at the coffee table, dressed in baggy gray sweatpants and a black hoodie. His dark hair was adorably tousled, and when he smiled at her, it held a warmth that made her insides squeeze.

"Sorry about that," she said, crossing the room to stand on the other side of the table, resting her hand on the back of a chair. It was awkward, clutching onto furniture, but it was better than occupying her hands in a way that betrayed her nervousness.

Sebastian smiled. "Don't be. I hope you enjoyed the view as much as I did."

Elena's cheeks heated, and her memory supplied a flash of Sebastian's sculpted backside. She shoved the image away and said, in a too-loud voice, "Are you baking?"

Sebastian folded his arms on top of the table. "Yeah. I couldn't sleep. Sorry if I woke you."

"No, I couldn't sleep either." She tapped her fingers on the back of the chair. "Why are you making bread?"

That warm smile again lighting up his face and making her stomach flutter. "I don't know. But I love the smell of freshly baked bread."

She nodded. "Me, too." She pulled out the chair opposite Sebastian and sat down, scooting her chair forward.

What now? What do you say to someone after seeing them naked?

Knowing what was beneath his baggy sweater did little to cool the warmth curling in her stomach. He'd filled out since she'd seen him naked last. The pale, skinny boy she'd loved was gone, replaced by a toned, muscular stranger.

"I, uh, like your condo," she said.

He chuckled. "Thanks. I like it too. That's why I bought it."

She could hear the teasing in his words, and it made her squirm.

Then the oven beeped, and they both rose, smacking their foreheads together. Elena thumped back, slid off her chair, and fell hard onto the floor.

"It's fine," she said, waving away Sebastian's hand. "Get the bread."

He nodded, then ran to the kitchen. She heard the oven opening and closing, a few short beeps, then a moment later, he clasped her hands and lifted her off the ground.

"So, how long before I can try your cooking?" she asked.

He grinned. "It needs to rest. Ideally, until tomorrow morning."

She groaned. "Come on. Really? But it smells so good."

She couldn't remember the last time she'd had homemade baked goods of any kind. Her mother had not been the kind to cook, and she'd never taken the time to learn.

"If milady insists." He gave her a short bow, then returned to the kitchen, where he tapped the pan upside down onto a cutting board. The bread thumped out, and Elena grabbed for it, but Sebastian smacked her hand with an oven mitt. "Not yet. It's too hot."

"What kind of bread is it?" She leaned closer and inhaled the savory smell of oregano and cheese. "It smells like pizza."

"That's because it's pizza bread. My mom always made it for us when we were kids. Don't you remember? Here." He twisted a chunk off the braided loaf with his gloved hands, then blew on it before handing it to her.

She took the piece in her fingers, tossing it from hand to hand until it was cool enough to handle, then sunk her teeth into it. It was soft, chewy, salty, and oh, so delicious. She finished the bite, then tapped Sebastian's forearm and held out her open palm when he looked at her.

"No more until morning," he said, crowding the bread with his body so she couldn't reach it. "You won't be able to sleep if you eat too much."

"I won't sleep either way," she said. "Come on. I'm hungry."

He sighed, then passed her another piece. This was better than the first, filled with small pieces of pepperoni and mushroom. As she licked the grease from her fingers, she caught his not-so-subtle shift away from her.

"Do you want a paper towel?" His voice was rough.

"No," Elena said. She stepped closer, then licked the middle finger of her right hand from her palm to the tip of her finger. "Mm, delicious."

"Is it?"

"See for yourself," she said, raising her hand to touch his lips with her fingertips.

Without breaking eye contact, Sebastian took her hand in one of his, folded three of her fingers down, then slipped her index finger into his mouth. His tongue rasped against her skin, and the sensation made her nipples tighten.

He drew her finger out of his mouth, then unfolded her fingers and kissed her palm.

"You're right," he murmured into her skin. "You are delicious."

She barely heard him over the beating of her heart in her ears.

What are you waiting for? Kiss him.

She wrapped her arms around his neck and brought their lips together. He stood as still as a statue, his arms at his side. After a moment of enjoying the warmth of his body, she pulled back.

"Isn't this what you wanted?" she whispered against his lips. "Tonight, I'm all yours."

She pressed her breasts against him and buried her nose in his neck. The rumbling in his chest reverberated through her body, and she took it as an encouragement to continue, grazing her teeth along the space where his shoulder met his neck. She bit lightly, then ran her tongue over the spot.

A hand crept beneath the waistband of her pants and cupped her rear. She squirmed, wanting to feel him inside her, and he obligingly drew his fingers down and dipped them between her legs. He slid his fingertips back and forth along her entrance before gently pressing inside. She arched her back and hissed in pleasure.

"Wait." He gently disengaged, then cupped her face and rubbed her cheeks with his thumbs. "Not like this." He touched his forehead to hers and sighed. "We're both exhausted."

She struggled out of his grip, pushing back angry tears. "Don't you want me?" She hated the whine in her words but could not stop it. The sting of his rejection lashed her heart like a whip.

"God—" He grasped her hips and drew her against his chest, tucking her head beneath his chin and squeezing her in a tight grip. The jut of his erection pressed against her stomach.

"Feel that? That's how much I want you." He released her and stepped away. "But we've both been through a traumatic day. I don't want you to make an emotional decision, then regret your choice tomorrow. When you come to me, I want you to be sure." He turned away, his shoulders heaving. "Good night, Elena."

"G-good night." She took a step back, almost knocked a cup off the counter, then turned and fled.

****

Sleep was no easier in coming to Elena, with the bread sitting like a brick in her stomach and the memory of Sebastian's lips tormenting her imagination. It was a heady feeling, knowing he was only a few feet away. She replayed the moment, his hands clasped around her hips, his tongue tangling with hers. He'd tasted like pizza, and his lips had been feather-light, like he expected her to shatter at the slightest touch. This was in stark contrast to the messy, wet kisses she'd shared with her past partners.

It was more than that, though. She felt safe with Sebastian so close. She longed to enter his room, crawl into his bed, cuddle against his chest, and feel his warmth surrounding her. The tension she lived with daily, which wrapped her in knots and had her jumping at every sound, was noticeably more bearable. He made her feel normal.

And now I've fucked it up.

Would he ever want her again after she'd thrown herself at him like a love-struck teenager?

Her pelvis was swollen and heavy, a sure sign she was in for a long and painful night. Her fingers fluttered over her nipples, and she imagined Sebastian's mouth there, his tongue rasping over her most sensitive areas.

He'd nuzzle her breasts, then kiss his way down her stomach to her—

What am I doing?

The thought of pleasuring herself with Sebastian sleeping a few feet away sent a fresh burst of heat to her core, and she squirmed, wishing she'd packed one of her vibrators. Unfortunately, she had not considered her sexual needs when putting together her get-out-of-dodge bag, and it was unlikely she'd ever be able to go back.

Well, one does what one must.

She slid her hands down her sides. Every slight movement made the old bed creak and groan.

He's right next door. He'll hear me.

She imagined Sebastian listening to the soft moans as she pleasured herself. Maybe he'd even join her, stroking himself with one hand while muffling his moans with a pillow. Was he imagining her as she imagined him?

Then something thudded in the hallway, and she stilled her hands, panting hard. Had he heard her? She remained completely still, but the condo was silent. With a sigh of relief, she began her movements anew, imagining Sebastian's coarse stubble brushing against her inner thigh. He'd slip two fingers inside her while rubbing her clit with his tongue.

Oh, God, Sebastian.

The pressure inside her pelvis grew but failed to crest. Tensing her muscles, she found the wave and rode it until her orgasm sizzled through her body and curled her toes. She rolled over to the cold side of the bed and tucked one of the extra pillows on the bed between her legs.

It would have to do.

****

It took a very long and cold shower to rid Sebastian

of the image of Elena sucking her finger with half-lidded eyes. Then, after toweling himself dry, he remembered the woman of his dreams was sleeping only a few feet away, and he was immediately hard again.

Groaning, he got into bed and tried not to think about her soft hair, the salty taste of her skin. The way she'd gasped when he'd touched her. The feeling of her tongue caressing the inside of his mouth.

Damn.

He growled his frustration and rolled onto his back. He hadn't imagined the way she'd toyed with him. She still had feelings for him, even after more than a decade apart.

Why the hell did I say no?

He flopped a hand over his face. It had seemed like the right thing to do. He didn't want her for a night; he wanted her forever.

Those soft brown eyes popped into his mind again, followed by the brief flash of delectable curves he'd gotten when she'd stumbled into the kitchen nude. The pale, stringy girl he'd been obsessed with as a young adult had blossomed into a true beauty.

This is mortifying.

It had been a very long time since he'd come so close to losing control. But that's what Elena did to him. She teased emotion out of him like a master.

With a silent apology to Elena, he indulged in a fantasy of seeing her spread beneath him, her dark hair splayed on his white sheets. The tension built until at last he found release.

Only then could he finally sleep.

Chapter 7

When Elena awoke the next morning, it took a moment to remember she was in Sebastian's guest bedroom. Then the events of the previous day flooded back, and her throat tightened.

Although her dream had started off pleasant—featuring a mostly naked Sebastian and an array of sliced fruits—it had quickly morphed into an endless repeat of Chloe's last memory as if to cement her resolve to find the killer.

She peeked beneath the blankets and confirmed Chloe was still with her, although the shade was coiled above her belly button. She tried again to reach for her friends' memories in her mind. It would've been a lot easier if she could just ask Chloe who had killed her. But there was nothing left of her friend but the chubby-bodied boa, an echo of who Chloe had once been

Elena pushed the forest-green blanket off her legs and smoothed her palm over the sheet beneath her, starched and crisp. She breathed in and smiled at the gentle scent of lavender with a hint of coffee. A distinct improvement over her apartment and the dingy motel room she'd almost slept in.

Her smile fell. She didn't belong in Stillwood. Eventually, the Harvester would catch up with her. By staying, she put Sebastian in danger. Still, her heart ached at the thought of leaving. The spark was still there.

It thrummed in her blood when he got too close, and she tasted it on his lips when they kissed. But when the time came, she would leave, as her mother had left. There was no point in thinking about what couldn't be.

She rolled out of bed.

To her left, the door opened to a long hallway. To her right, a sturdy oak chest stood in stark contrast to the white walls. She opened the chest and removed the change of clothes she'd shoved in the previous night, a maroon V-neck that fit snug against her midriff, dark blue jeans, and a sweater.

Then her bladder reminded her she had slept late. She returned to the bathroom, then flicked the empty roll of toilet paper. In pursuit of another bathroom, she followed the aroma of coffee to the kitchen, where Sebastian was rummaging through the fridge. "Morning," she called and received a muffled greeting in reply. "Where's your bathroom?"

He frowned. "There's one attached to the spare bedroom?"

"No toilet paper."

Sebastian winced and pointed to the left. "Down the hall. First door on your left. Sorry, it's been a while since I've had a guest."

Elena followed the hall and found a small bathroom. As she entered, a prickling swept up her legs, followed by the sound of distant giggling. Then she was ousted from her body with a feeling like jumping off a swing at its highest arc, except instead of falling onto gravel on her knees, she floated up and away.

Get out of my body!

Elena mentally pushed against the force that had displaced her. It didn't help. The shade—Where had she picked it up?—was too strong. She collapsed beneath the weight of its will.

She pushed through the bustling crowds of afternoon commuters on Main Street, her heart pounding in her chest.

The man was following her.

Even though she hadn't seen him, his gaze was like a brand on her skin. Every time she turned a corner, she expected him to be there, ready to thrust a knife between her ribs.

Why hadn't he killed her yet?

The scene faded, leaving Elena to watch the shade lean over the vanity. Her body breathed out, fogging the mirror. A shaking finger touched the glass and, in halting movements, spelled out the word *Help*.

Help who? Who are you? What do you want?

She reached for the shade's presence again, but it shied away, and as the marks faded, so did the pressure against Elena's mind. She was sucked back into her body so abruptly that she didn't orient properly like she'd shoved both feet into the same pant leg and gotten stuck. When the sensation passed, she carefully searched her skin, but the only shade she carried was Chloe's boa, sitting sedately on her stomach.

"Was that you?"

The boa stuck out its forked tongue.

"I'll take that as a no."

Whatever shade had taken her over was long gone, hopefully forever.

She resisted the urge to scream or cry. Maybe both. Instead, she pulled out her phone and dialed a number with shaking fingers.

The phone clicked, and a voice answered. "Hello?"

Her shoulders relaxed. "Hey, Aunt Martha, it's me."

"Hello, dear." A brief pause. "Are you okay?"

Elena stared at her reflection in the mirror, remembering the word the shade had written. "Yes. No. I'm not sure. I just had a strange encounter."

Her aunt's voice hardened. "What kind of encounter?"

"I was possessed, out of nowhere, but then the shade wrote the word *Help* on the mirror, then released control. I think it was trying to send me a message."

Her aunt sighed. "How often are you being possessed?"

"This was the first time in weeks," Elena said, crushing a twinge of guilt at the lie. "Why? Why does that matter?"

Her aunt hummed. "Mr. Castillo didn't see you like that, did he?"

"I—what? No. Of course not."

It was difficult enough explaining her odd behavior to strangers. She couldn't lie to Sebastian. He'd see through her like a pane of glass.

"Wait," Elena said, rolling back the tape of their conversation in her head. "How do you know where I am?"

"I have my ways."

"You know what, never mind. I'll figure this out on my own."

She hung up, put her phone away, then traced the word on the mirror.

Who are you? What do you want from me?

She looked at the mirror for another few seconds, then decided the best thing to do was put the entire ordeal out of her mind. She had enough to deal with without worrying about the problems of shades.

She relieved her physical needs, then indulged her curiosity and checked the rest of the doors in the hall. One was a linen closet with blankets, sheets, towels— she took two of each—and an unopened package of toilet paper. She tore it open and took three. After depositing her bounty back in her room, her stomach urged her back to the kitchen.

Sebastian stood in the middle of the room, his mouth open, his eyes cloudy black.

She froze, expecting to hear a grating voice. But then he threw a piece of cheese in the air and caught it in his mouth.

"Hey, look at that, still got it," he said. Then he blinked. "What's wrong?"

She shook off the chains of fear. "Nothing. What's for breakfast?"

He chuckled. "There's not much but help yourself."

She grabbed a piece of pizza bread and a container of sliced white cheese from the fridge. She took an experimental bite of cheese and hummed in pleasure. It was cheddar, expensive, with the tang of age.

Sebastian sat at the table, then opened a thin laptop. "Other than the toilet paper, is everything okay with the room?"

"It's perfect," she said. "Thanks again for letting me stay."

He returned to his typing. "There was no way I was going to let you stay at the Hamilton. It was grungy fifteen years ago. Now it's a total dive."

Elena took the chair opposite Sebastian, then fiddled with her phone.

I guess we aren't talking about last night.

That was fine with her. No matter how her heart ached, it was a bad idea to get attached. Whenever she got complacent, all she had to do was summon the image of her mother leaning over Edward, a knife clutched in her hands, possessed by a psychotic shade. Her mother, the strongest woman she'd ever met.

I'll never let that happen to me.

For a while, they kept a pact of silence. He typed on his keyboard, muttering beneath his breath, and she scrolled through various social media feeds on her phone. It was a pleasant change, a normal morning. She imagined what it would be like to live like everyone else. Having breakfast with Sebastian. Discussing their plans for the day. Laughing about not wanting to go back to work. Wrapping her arms around his neck, kissing him silly.

Then her phone rang, disrupting her fantasy.

Sebastian looked up from his typing and raised an eyebrow.

"It's my lawyer," she said. She was surprised he had taken so long to call her but better late than never. She held the phone to her ear.

"Hey."

"Elena? Are you okay?" David asked. "I got a call earlier saying you were in the police station, asking for me."

She flushed. "Sorry about that. There was an unexpected incident." She cleared her throat. "I came back to check out the house, but when I arrived, there was a body floating in the pool."

"A *what*?" David groaned. "Please tell me you didn't talk to the cops."

"We-ell," She hadn't said much, but certainly more

than she should've.

Another groan. "Okay. Don't say another word until I arrive. I'll be back in two days, three at the most."

Two days?

"Where are you now?"

It was unlike David to leave his cushy office in downtown Minneapolis. The old man was stubbornly proud of his work ethic, and she'd never known him to take a vacation.

"Wisconsin," David said. "It's a long story. I've got to run, remember—"

"Don't talk to the cops," she repeated. "I get it. I'll see you in a few days. Bye."

David said goodbye, then the line disconnected. Elena lowered it and was about to put it back into her pocket when it started vibrating again. She rolled her eyes and answered.

"What now, David?"

"She—You—" Between the words were bursts of static, and the voice was certainly not David's. She looked at her phone screen but didn't recognize the number.

Sebastian closed the lid of his laptop. "Put it on speakerphone."

She did and then winced at the static.

"Get out," a distorted voice said. "Get out!"

Her legs trembled, and a wave of cold washed over her.

Sebastian pushed away from the table and walked around to stand behind her, placing his hands on her shoulders. She looked up into his concerned expression, then leaned over and spoke into the phone as if her insides didn't feel like jelly. "Who is this?"

"You don't belong here," the voice said.

A strangled whimper escaped her throat. Sebastian squeezed her shoulders, and Elena mustered up her courage. When she spoke again, her voice no longer held a tremor. "That's not funny."

A few seconds of silence, then the voice returned, harsher this time. "Leave before you get someone else killed."

Click.

Elena put her phone on the table, face up. "They hung up. Do you think that was…" She couldn't finish the sentence. Saying it out loud opened possibilities she didn't want to acknowledge.

The killer knows who you are.

He wants you to leave.

He'll come after you next.

"What am I going to do?" Elena moaned.

Sebastian wrapped an arm around her shoulders and rested his cheek on her head.

"We'll figure it out." He pressed a kiss to her hair. "I won't let anything happen to you. I promise." Then he let go and found his coat and keys. "Come on, there's someone you need to meet."

Chapter 8

Sebastian clenched his hands around the wheel and kept his gaze on the license plate of the SUV in front of him. "All I'm saying is, you have to be more careful. Someone obviously has it out for you."

Most of the drive had been spent arguing with his unruly passenger, and it had frayed his usually steady temper to the breaking point. Against her wishes, he'd called the station and reported both the goggles in her bag and the threatening phone call. As expected, Roth had dismissed his concerns, insisting the local kids were getting a thrill out of torturing the daughter of the countess of death.

He glanced into the rear-view mirror. He had no intention of allowing Elena to learn her mother's gruesome nickname.

"Do you really think it was the killer who called?" Elena asked.

"We have to assume it was," he replied "The question is, why are they targeting you? Did you see anyone yesterday before I arrived at the house?"

She was quiet for a few moments, then said, "No. I didn't see anything out of the ordinary when I arrived."

There had to be a reason the killer had targeted her. The urge to take an exit onto the interstate and drive until they ran out of gas rocked him. He had a couple hundred dollars in cash. They could stay at a motel and wait for the danger to pass.

You just want to be in a room alone with her again.

He remembered how she'd leaned into his arms, whispering promises of pleasure. It had taken all his willpower not to take her there, against the kitchen wall.

He indulged in a silent fantasy of having her spread beneath him on his bed, her dark hair fanned out on the pillows, her lips curved in a seductive smile. He shifted his legs. It was going to be a long drive.

By the time they arrived at the tall brownstone in the outer boroughs of Minneapolis, Elena was all but vibrating with impatience. They exited the car, and then she dragged him along by the arm to the elevator, then trailed behind him as they walked down the hallway. He found the correct door, then knocked.

A chubby woman with curling brown hair opened the door and grinned at them.

Elena gasped. "You!"

Sebastian looked between the two women. "You've met?"

"I'll explain later," Elena murmured.

"You look like you just crawled out of the grave," Sandra said, leaning against the door frame. She wore a gray sweater and navy sweatpants. "Well, let's get this over with." She ushered them onto the couch in the sunken living room. Boxes of computer parts filled the table. In the corner, a TV was paused on an old episode of a popular British Sci-Fi show.

Sandra touched the top of the television, and it flickered, then turned off. Then she put her hands on her hips. "What's wrong with you, letting this poor woman run herself ragged. Shame on you."

She looked around the room. "Clear off the table.

I'll get some tea. As my grandmother used to say, a good host always offers tea."

Before he could defend himself, she retreated into the kitchen, and then tinny, upbeat music started playing. He picked up two boxes of computer parts on the coffee table, one under each arm, and relocated them to the corner, where other boxes lay, their contents spilled out onto the floor in a tangle of cords and metal.

When there was enough space freed, they sat on the couch.

"When did you meet Sandra?" he asked.

"At the station yesterday. She, uh, rescued me. Then she made me help her steal something out of evidence."

The image of Sandra pulling Elena along by the hand through the police station corridors made him smile.

"Her father's the sheriff," he said.

Elena scratched behind her ear. "And that explains it, how?"

He chuckled. "They've got an ongoing battle. Sandra tests their security. She believes if she can break in, someone else can."

Sandra had always toed the line of the law, even with a father in law enforcement. But as far as he knew, she'd never stepped over that line.

Had something changed?

There was a loud clanging of dishes from the kitchen, then Sandra returned, bearing a tray with tea and cookies. Elena straightened at the sight, like a dog after hearing the word "treat." He laughed, then laughed harder when Sandra scowled.

"I'm sorry," he said. "Tea and cookies?"

Sandra lifted the tray off the table. "I guess I'll put

these away then."

Elena elbowed him in the ribs, hard.

"Ah, well," he coughed. "What I meant to say is, what a wonderful gesture. We'd love tea and cookies."

"All right then," Sandra said. She put the tray back down and wiped her forehead with her sleeve. "Lord, it's hot in here." She slipped off her sweater and draped it over the back of her chair.

Elena dropped a cookie, showering the carpet with crumbs, then clutched his arm.

"What is it?" he studied her pale face. "What's wrong?"

She opened her mouth and emitted a gurgling sound. *Is she choking?*

He shot Sandra a concerned look and slapped Elena on the back a few times, but she didn't react. Then she shot to her feet, crouching over with her hands fisted near her chest, and squinted. "What is this? Who're you, sonny? What're you doing with my granddaughter?"

He choked out a laugh. "What is that, an impression? I don't get the reference." He looked at Sandra, who was just as pale as Elena. Sandra shook her head back and forth but said nothing.

What the hell is going on?

Elena shuffled forward, toddling like an eighty-year-old woman. "Listen here, sonny—"

She cut off mid-sentence with a choking sound and then straightened. "Uh, yeah, something I saw on TV. Sorry, I thought you'd get it." She wiped the sheen of sweat from her face with a napkin from the table, then fell back onto the couch beside him.

"Oh!" Sandra said. "Yes, I get it!" She laughed, although it sounded strained. "You must be tired. Have some tea." She lifted the blue teapot and filled the three matching cups.

Sebastian accepted the cup she held out to him "Thanks."

Sandra sipped from her cup, then eyed him. "When you called, you said it was urgent. What's going on?"

He put his cup down without trying the tea. "Elena got a weird call about an hour ago. I was hoping you could help us figure out where it came from."

Sandra had been apt with technology for as long as he could remember. They'd met in college when he'd still been keen on joining the force. He'd helped her move out of her apartment after her boyfriend had knocked her around. She'd helped him sort out a stolen credit card that had caused Chloe some grief.

Sandra shook her head. "It doesn't work that way."

"Can't you just," he mimed a typing motion. "Make it happen?"

Sandra rolled her eyes. "This isn't a movie. I'm not just going to hack into some city database and find the answers you're looking for."

Elena paused her eating to chime in. "But you could? If you wanted to?"

"Sure. If that data even existed. But I'm not going to. It's dangerous, Bast. I don't take risks like that, not unless there's a damn good reason." Sandra stopped him from interrupting with a gesture. "A prank call is not a good reason."

Sebastian slumped in his seat. "Damn."

"What do we do now?" Elena picked up another cookie. "Go back to the condo?"

"I can't just sit around and do nothing," Sebastian said. "My sister's killer is out there, and Roth is so focused on me as a suspect, he is probably not investigating anyone else."

"It's simple, then," Elena said. "We'll have to do his job for him."

Sandra made a whooping noise. "Amateur detectives! Count me in." She grabbed something from behind her chair and held it up in the air. "Surprise!"

He gaped. "How did you get that?"

"Let's just say you owe me. Big time."

Elena stared at the object in Sandra's hands. "Isn't that the laptop you took out of evidence?"

"Not just any laptop," Sebastian said. "Chloe's laptop. I'd recognize those stickers anywhere."

Sandra relocated to an office chair in front of a desk. "If your sister was into something, there may be evidence on here." She took a large black contraption out of a drawer and put it on her desk.

"What are you doing?" Sebastian asked.

"We can't just plug it into one of my computers," Sandra said. She unscrewed the hard drive and slotted it into the contraption. "That's called tampering with evidence. But a cloned hard drive isn't the same. As long as we're careful." She gestured to the computer tower under her desk. "I use this machine for forensics." Then she launched into a complicated explanation of what she planned to do. He couldn't pretend to understand half of what she said, but he nodded along. When she eventually trailed off, occupied with setting up her equipment, he turned to Elena. "Do you want to see this?"

She shook her head. "You do the tech stuff. I'm famished."

He laughed. "Are you ever not hungry?"

Elena picked up another cookie, met his eyes, and

shoved the entire thing in her mouth.

"There's some chicken fingers and fries on top of the oven," Sandra said from beneath her desk. "I was about to have lunch when you called. Help yourself. I cooked them in the air fryer."

Elena raced out of the room like rabid dogs were on her tail.

"Oh, lord." Sandra wiped tears of mirth from her eyes. "She's precious. I see why you like her. Now, Come. Watch. Maybe you'll learn something."

"I doubt that. But I'll watch, anyway."

Their first pass of the files on the drive was not revealing. He soon lost track as Sandra clicked around the screen, navigating through windows faster than he could follow.

Then Elena turned the corner, half-eaten chicken finger in her hand. "Did you find anything?"

Sandra beamed. "Nope! Looks like she wiped the drive a few days ago. I've got a restore program running, but it might take a while to finish."

Sebastian thumped down on the couch.

So much for that.

"We need to trace her last steps," Sebastian said. "Find out what she was doing over the past few days. Maybe that will give us a clue."

"Ah! That I can help you with," Sandra said. "Come, marvel at my genius." She pranced over to the couch and sat down, then waved at Elena and patted the cushions beside her.

Sebastian leaned over Sandra's shoulder. She held her phone with a map program open in a browser.

"What is this, directions?" he asked.

Sandra tapped on the corner of the screen, where a

circular icon showed a roaring lion. "Chloe's account. She had location tracking on, so we can see where she has been. Or, more accurately, where her phone has been. Let's start the day she died." She tapped around the screen. Blue lines traced Chloe's movement from town to the Cain house.

"Not much," Sebastian said. "Although I didn't see her phone on her body."

Sandra hummed a sound. "She was in the water, right? If she had her phone on her, it probably died. Let's check the day before." She touched an arrow, and the screen changed, the lines spreading out across Stillwood. "Restaurant, hair salon, bowling alley, restaurant, grocery store," Sandra said, scrolling through the page. "Busy girl, Chloe." She touched a button, and the blue lines vanished.

"What happened?" he grabbed the phone. "Did someone wipe out the data?"

Sandra twisted the device out of his grip. "It's nothing. She just didn't go anywhere that day. Or at least, her phone didn't."

The screen changed again, showing another pattern of blue lines.

"Grocery store, restaurant, bowling alley."

The screen changed for a third time.

"Can you slow down a bit?" Elena groaned. "You're making me queasy."

Sandra grinned at her. "Lightweight."

Then Sebastian poked at the screen. "Look, the bowling alley again."

"Was she part of a league or something?" Elena asked.

"Not that I know of," Sebastian said. "The hobbies

she enjoyed were more things you can do at home—reading, watching TV, stuff like that."

Sandra clicked on the bowling alley and brought up a new page that included photos of the interior, business hours, and more. She clicked on the link to a website, then rapidly scrolled down several screen lengths before stopping. "There's no league playing right now, anyway." She tapped the screen with her fingernail. "See? The season starts up next month."

"Why would she be going there so often?" Sebastian resisted the urge to grab the phone. Chloe's movements didn't make sense. What had she been up to?

Sandra shrugged. "I just dig up the data. It's up to you to decide what to do with it."

As if sensing the guilt that had settled over him, Elena wrapped an arm around his shoulders and squeezed.

"It's a lead," Sebastian said. "I say we check it out."

Chapter 9

What was Chloe doing here?

Elena rolled down her window to better see the bowling alley through the parking lot. It was in the basement of a strip mall, with large trees overhanging the stairs. Plastic bags tangled in the tree branches rustled in the wind, and discarded coffee cups tumbled down the sidewalk and settled in the gutters. A battered *For Lease* sign hid behind a windowpane of the store above the alley. No phone number, just the words *Inquire Within* scrawled in ink.

They watched the building for a while, but after seeing only young couples and the occasional uniformed bowler descend the stairs to Valley Lanes, they exited the car and made their way down. A frosted glass door met them at the bottom. When Sebastian opened it, the smell of popcorn and stale beer wreathed around them. Inside, the lights were dim, and lasers in the ceiling made patterns on the floor. Their white clothing glowed neon under the black lights and the sound of pins clattering filled the air.

They passed an empty front counter and found a small dining area to the left of the lanes.

"Now it makes sense," Sebastian said, pointing to a sign advertising authentic Mexican cuisine. "She loved finding hole-in-the-wall restaurants. I bet the food here is amazing."

"Mystery solved, I guess," Elena said. She was about to propose they leave when her stomach growled.

"Don't even start," she said, hearing Sebastian wheeze. "Come on. Might as well eat now that we're here." She hooked his arm in hers and walked over to the *Please wait to be seated* sign separating the carpeted area from the laminated floor beneath the restaurant tables.

A young woman in a black smock looked up from behind a pedestal and asked if they wanted a table or a booth, then led them to a quiet booth in the corner. Elena ordered *chilaquiles*, ignoring Sebastian's muted laughter. He ordered coffee and a *carne asada torta*.

When the server left, Elena slid the ceramic dish in the center of the table toward her. It was crammed with a disorganized mess of sugar packets. She dumped it on the table and started sorting them by color.

"Something isn't adding up," Sebastian said. "Why would Chloe come here several days in a row? I can't imagine the food being that good. She got bored with new things quickly." He clicked his tongue. "I have an idea. Follow my lead."

He moved one bottle on their table to the floor, then leaned over to smile at the elderly couple sitting in the booth beside them. "Excuse me, can we borrow your hot sauce?"

"Of course," the woman said. She handed over the bottle.

Sebastian looked at Elena and raised his eyebrows. It took her another few seconds to understand his plan. She copied his pose and smiled at the couple. "Come here often?"

"Oh yes," the woman said as her partner finished up the last of his steak and eggs. "Albert and I are regulars.

We had our first date here." She clasped hands with her partner, and they smiled into each other's eyes.

What would it be like to have that kind of relationship? To grow into old age together.

It was a painful thought because she knew it could never happen. The odds were, she wouldn't live long enough for it to become a reality.

"You okay?" Sebastian placed his hand on top of hers on the table.

She plastered on a fake smile and slipped her hand away. "Yes, of course. Why don't you ask these nice people about your sister? Maybe they'll know something."

The woman brightened. "Oh?"

"Ah, yes," Sebastian continued. "She's been avoiding us, and we're worried. We know she's been here a few times in the last week. Tall woman, striking green eyes, looks like a model?"

Albert laughed. "Oh, my yes. We've seen her."

The couple looked at each other and smiled. Then the woman laughed. "I'm sorry. It's just she always comes here alone, then meets with a man. We have a private joke that the man is her handler, and she is a secret agent. We like to make up stories for other diners." She pointed to a far corner of the restaurant. "She usually sits over there, orders a black coffee and *huevos rancheros* with extra salsa. I told her that cheese will go right to her thighs, but she laughed and said she could afford the calories." The woman gasped. "Oh, I'm sorry. How rude of me. My name is Henrietta."

As Sebastian did the polite thing and introduced them, Elena's mind swam. Chloe had been meeting with someone.

The killer?

No, that wouldn't make sense. Why meet with the killer and in such a public place?

Unless she didn't realize he was the killer.

If she'd gotten close to someone, it might explain why she had felt so betrayed in her final memory.

It would be great if you could tell me if we're on the right track, Chloe.

The last she'd checked, the boa rested on her stomach. She reached for the sparkle of Chloe's shade in her mind, but it shied away from her, revealing nothing.

"We appreciate your help," Sebastian said.

They paused as their server arrived with their food. When they finished, Sebastian looked over the booth again. "This man you've seen my sister with. What does he look like?"

Henrietta leaned forward. "I'm not sure. He always sits away from us and wears a hat, coat, and sunglasses. He doesn't bowl or even order food, just shows up, talks for a few minutes, then leaves. It's all very mysterious. Scandalous even."

Sebastian gasped. "Oh, my. I wonder if my sister is in trouble?"

Henrietta clasped Sebastian's hands in her own. "Oh, dear. I wish I could tell you more. When I see her again, should I say something?"

"Oh, that's okay," Sebastian said. He met Elena's eyes and nodded to the front desk.

She took the hint and spoke up. "We should leave soon, dear, or we'll be late for our movie."

Henrietta nodded. "Well, it was so nice meeting you. I hope everything goes well with your sister."

Sebastian flagged down their server and got their

bill, then paid with a fifty he casually took out of his wallet.

I wonder how much cash he carries with him.

The spike of jealousy was unwelcome, but her whole life had been lived in poverty, from her mother's meager server salary to whatever she could make in the few months she stayed in any city.

"What's wrong?" Sebastian stood and shrugged on his coat. "Meal not agree with you? Or did you finally eat too much, for once?"

"Impossible," she said. Then, in a lower voice, "I was thinking about Chloe's movements. They don't make sense. Why meet with a man in a bowling alley? What did he have to do with anything?"

Sebastian shook his head. "I don't know. But whoever this man is, I'm sure he's involved."

They exited through the frosted doors and ran straight into Detective Roth at the base of the stairs.

"Ms. Cain. Castillo," Roth said. "I think it's time we had another talk."

"What do you want?" Sebastian stepped between the man and Elena.

A muscle in Roth's jaw twitched. "Not here. At the station."

Elena remembered David's advice about not talking to cops, and she shook her head. "We're not talking to you without my lawyer."

Roth's eyes narrowed to slits before he relaxed and adopted an easy smile. "We got off on the wrong foot, Ms. Cain. For that, I apologize. Chloe was important to me." His eyes grew misty, but then he blinked, and his eyes were clear again. "Regardless, I shouldn't have taken out my anger on either of you. It was unprofessional."

"Apology accepted," Sebastian said in a deadpan voice. "Is that all? We've got things to do."

Roth's jaw twitched again, but he stepped out of their way. As they passed, he said, "We both want the same thing, you know. To find whoever killed your sister."

Sebastian kept climbing the stairs, but she hooked her hand around his arm and pulled him back. As little as she trusted cops, Roth had a point. They were harming the investigation by not sharing what they'd discovered.

Sebastian leaned toward her and whispered, "Don't tell him anything."

"I think he really wants to help," she whispered back.

Then Roth cleared his throat and said, "I can hear you; you know."

Now or never.

She summoned her nerve and pushed away from Sebastian. "We think Chloe was searching for something. She had—she was—" Belatedly, she remembered they had got their clues from Sandra's hacking into Chloe's phone.

"My sister had gotten really interested in bowling lately," Sebastian finished.

Elena glared at him, then added, "She was meeting someone here on the regular. We don't know who or why."

Roth took a notebook and pen out of his pocket and flipped to a new page, then scribbled. "Anything else?"

Elena's bravado fizzled out. "No, that's it."

Roth tapped his closed notebook against his palm three times, then sighed. "Okay. I know what you two are doing, and although I can't approve of amateur sleuthing, the truth is we could use the help. So, this is what I know." He searched through his notebook and flipped it open to a page. "We've had a string of drownings in the last six months. In each case, there were indications of strangulation prior to death." He closed his notebook. "If you ask me, it's the same person responsible."

"You're talking about a serial killer," Sebastian said.

"Yes." Roth gave them a pained expression. "But please don't go talking to the press about this."

"We won't tell anyone," Elena said, quickly. "Thank you for trusting us with that information. We'll do our best to stay out of your way."

"Don't let me stop you," Roth said dryly. Then he turned and ascended the steps.

They followed him, parting at the top of the steps and returning to their car. Once they were inside and buckled in, Sebastian slouched over and rested his head on the wheel. "I should've stopped her. Why didn't I stop her? I knew she was getting in too deep. She showed me the autopsy photographs, for fucks sake!" He slammed his head on the wheel, and the horn honked.

Nothing she could say would change how he felt. All she could do was be with him. She threaded her fingers through his.

The moment was interrupted by a thumping on their window.

It was Sandra, grinning at them. She jumped into the backseat and said, "The hard drive finished restoring."

Elena leaned around her seat. "What did you find?"

"Nothing!" Sandra said with a huge smile.

Elena looked at Sebastian, who shrugged.

"You don't get it. Of course. Sorry. Let me explain." She cleared her throat. "There was nothing because Chloe had a storage device attached to the computer. That's where all her files will be."

Storage device?

"Like a USB stick?" Elena thought back to her high school days.

"Maybe. Could be anything," Sandra said. "As small as a micro-SD card." She pinched her fingers together. "Or as large as an external hard drive." She held her hands out a few inches apart, in the shape of a book.

"Should we tell the cops?" Elena thought of how forthcoming Roth had been.

Sebastian barked a laugh. "I think by now we know we can't trust the cops."

"I have to agree," Sandra said. "I love my father, but I don't trust him."

"Why don't we check her house?" Elena asked. "Maybe we can find more clues there."

Sebastian shook his head. "I don't have the keys. She was renting. I could call the office and ask, but—"

Sandra coughed. "Leave that to me."

Chapter 10

Rain pattered against the roof of the car, streaming down the windshield and casting the world in a blurry haze. The leather seat was stiff and chilly beneath Elena's thin jeans. She clenched the passenger side door handle. The sharp plastic edges dug into her skin.

"Are you sure this car has enough clearance?" she surveyed the flooded road before them. She was about to suggest turning around when a beige minivan sped past them, throwing up a tidal wave of water that crashed over the car. Sebastian muttered obscenities, and Elena flashed the driver an obscene gesture.

A light turned red ahead of them. Sebastian hit the brake too hard, and the car skidded sideways. Elena whipped her head around. The car behind them swerved into the other lane and sped through the intersection, missing an oncoming truck by inches.

From the back seat, Sandra clapped her hands and laughed. "This is the most fun I've had in ages!"

"Don't encourage him," Elena said. At the same time, she wondered about the change in Sebastian's behavior. As kids, he'd been the voice of reason, talking them down from whatever scheme Chloe cooked up.

What changed?

They continued driving at a more sedate pace until they spotted the turnoff. Elena closed her eyes in silent relief. Her stress levels were high enough without having to worry about rolling into the ditch.

The rain worsened, a deafening chorus of water hitting the roof of the car. Elena leaned closer to the windshield. There was a brick building across the road. The white front door was protected from the deluge by a small awning.

Sebastian parked across the street, unbuckled his seat belt, removed the keys from the ignition, and then stared at them in his hand.

The clouds parted and allowed a thin stream of sunlight. Sandra's head popped up between the seats. "Well? Are we going in or what? I've got other things to do today, you know."

Elena leaned over the seat and raised her eyebrows.

"Oh," Sandra said. "I'll go get started without you." Then she hurried out of the car and raced across the road.

Elena turned to Sebastian, and his expression made her heart cry out in sympathy.

"It's my fault she's dead," he said, staring at the keys in his hand. "If I'd showed up a few minutes earlier—" He clenched his fingers around the keys. "I don't know if I can go in there."

"This is not your fault," Elena said, willing him to believe it. "There is nothing you could have done. Chloe loved you. She was lucky to have you as a brother."

For a moment, his eyes glossed over. But the next second, his expression shuttered, and he turned away, pulling his hand from her grasp.

"You're wrong," he said. He closed his eyes, and his throat worked. "She loved Edward, not me."

The pattering slowed and stopped, and Elena spied a dark shape hurrying toward the car. She grasped for the door handle before recognizing Sandra.

The back door opened, and Sandra leapt inside. She slicked back her hair and pulled her phone out of her pocket. "There we go. Commercial locks are a piece of cake."

Elena rooted around the car for a towel or napkin, but when she saw the ride share app open on Sandra's phone, she stopped. "Wait, you're not coming?"

Sandra shook her head, tapping on her phone. "Nah. I've got to work on Chloe's laptop. Plus," she clicked the power button and slid her phone back into her pocket. "I'm dying for a hot shower. My ride will be here in fifteen."

****

Elena shimmied through the door of the house, pushing away the cats twining around her legs, crying for attention. She made it inside and hooked the cats under each arm so Sebastian could enter.

The house was open concept in design. The kitchen separated from the living room by a tall island surrounded by metal stools. Three cream leather couches surrounded a varnished oak coffee table on top of a finely woven Arabic rug. Jutting off to the side was a hallway that presumably led to the bedrooms and bathrooms.

"It's… nice," Elena said, dropping the cats to the ground. The home didn't feel like a space Chloe would have decorated. It was too cold. Sterile.

"I know. It doesn't feel like her," Sebastian said. His pocket vibrated, and he pulled out his phone, then grimaced. "Sorry, I have to take this." He clicked the accept button and held the phone to his head. "Hello?" He opened a door that led down into the basement and descended. "Slow down. I can't understand you." He closed the door behind him, and his voice faded.

When he didn't return after a few minutes, Elena explored the house. The kitchen was modern with white cabinets, white appliances, and white tile. The abundance of white reminded her of a hospital.

The larger of the cats, an orange and white striped tom, thumped to his side and stared at her over the mound of his stomach. The other, a gray domestic medium hair, stepped onto a discarded paper bag and watched her with piercing green eyes.

A photo on the fridge supplied a clue to their names. In the picture, Chloe held a gray cat against a starry background. It looked like something a student would get for a graduation photo. She stifled a snicker. The cat looked less than pleased. She flipped the picture over. The words Chloe and Silky, 2013 were printed on the back in red ink. She glanced at the orange ball of fluff on the kitchen floor. "Who are you then?"

The cat's gaze provided no answers. She ruffled his head. "I'll call you Tiger."

Then she turned to the gray cat and touched the paper bag with her toe. "That would make you Silky."

Silky swatted at her toe.

Food before cuddles. Got it.

She opened the cabinets until she found a section devoted to the cats. A pricking on her thigh had her looking down to see Silky reaching up her leg, claws extended.

"Play nice. I'm a visitor." She shook the cat loose. Silky settled onto her paws, watching her through lidded eyes.

She took a can of cat food at random from the cabinet and pulled the tab. A pungent smell filled the room. She retched, but the cats perked up, meowing at her. She fetched a bowl and tapped the can until it expelled the mass with a wet, slapping sound. Then she emptied a second can into another bowl. Silky jumped onto the counter and pawed at the food. Tiger meowed from the floor, and she petted his head. When the second bowl hit the floor, he turned up his nose and strutted away.

Typical.

With the cats sorted, she walked out of the kitchen and scanned the photos on the wall.

Chloe and Elena standing side by side, grinning with mouths full of metal on the day they'd both gotten braces. Chloe showing off the red dress she'd worn to their first middle school dance, the hem uneven from where she'd tried to raise it herself. Years flew by as Chloe grew from awkward teen to elegant young woman. In the later pictures, she looked like a model with her vibrant green eyes, light brown skin, and long, wavy hair.

Thump.

The door at the end of the hall was closed, but light flickered beneath. A shadow passed. She slapped a hand over her mouth and considered retreating, calling Sebastian or the police.

But what if it's the killer here to remove evidence?

If so, she owed it to Chloe to stop him. She padded closer, then touched her fingertips against the door and pushed until the gap was large enough to see through. Inside, a tall figure dressed in black yanked clothes from a dresser onto the floor. He muttered to himself, although she couldn't catch the words.

Looking for Chloe's hard drive?

Then the man turned and walked toward the door. A

ski mask obscured most of his features, but he wore a short-sleeved shirt, and there was a shade on his arm. It was a gigantic wolf spider. She shuddered.

Why must it always be spiders?

The man hurried toward her. She cursed and stepped through the nearest doorway, then closed the door as softly as she could.

The walls of the closet loomed around her.

"No, no, no," she whispered, a band tightening around her chest. Fifteen years of therapy hadn't cured the claustrophobia she'd struggled with since that night.

With shaking hands, she retrieved her phone from her pocket, then remembered she'd turned it off to save power. If she turned it on again, the man outside would hear the noise. She'd left it on full volume.

She closed her eyes and ignored the pounding in her ears. The walls pulsed, threatening to squeeze her into submission. Her arm hit a pile of boxes, and they tumbled over.

More shuffling, drawers opening and closing. She forced herself to remain still. Then prickling started in her fingers and rushed up her arms.

Please, not now!

She fought back, holding her breath against the pressure in her mind. But her fear was a chink in her armor, and she was unceremoniously tossed from her body. She reached toward the consciousness sharing her body, but it shied away from her. A second later, cold tendrils drew her into one of her own memories.

She kicked off her sneakers and tossed her school backpack to the floor.

"I'm home!" she called, reaching back with a foot to catch the closing door.

She missed. It slammed shut behind her, and she cringed. "Sorry," she yelled. "I tried to catch it!"

Silence filled the house once again, making her nervous. Why was her mother not yelling at her for letting the door slam?

She shoved a handful of nuts from the bowl on the front landing into her mouth. The house was quiet, unusual for a weekday.

There was a murmuring from somewhere in the house, the words indecipherable.

"Mom?" she whispered. Fear was a live thing inside her, wrapping around her insides and squeezing.

Her mouth dried, and the nuts solidified to a bitter mass. She swallowed, bitterness filling her mouth. Her ears strained to decipher words from the murmuring noise.

She tiptoed up the stairs and peeked around the corner into the hallway. Her mother stood in her bedroom, talking to someone she couldn't see.

"Mom?"

Her mother raised her arm. Clasped in her hand was a knife.

Elena staggered closer. Edward kneeled on the floor, holding up his arms, tears running down his face.

"Mom, what're you doing?" she asked before she could stop herself.

Her mother's head jerked around like a clockwork toy. Her face was twisted, her lips curled in a snarl, and her eyes were completely black.

"Filthy child," she rasped, her voice low and distorted. "Get out of here, or I'll take care of you next!"

Elena slipped into the hall closet, pressed her hands over her ears, and screamed until her throat was raw.

The memory faded away, leaving Elena to watch the shade operating her body. It pawed her pockets, found her phone, and then held the power button.

Shit, not that! He'll hear!

As if understanding the danger, the shade balled up the phone in her shirt, rolling the fabric until it was cocooned, then crouched over to muffle the sound. The vibration tickled her stomach, then the shade unrolled the phone, unlocked it—why hadn't she turned off that security setting?—and opened a note-taking app. With rapid strokes, using the slide-to-type feature that Elena had never mastered, the shade wrote four words in all capital letters.

FIND RESEARCH STOP HIM

Then the pressure the shade exerted on Elena's mind dissipated, and the resulting vacuum sucked her back into her body. This time, she was prepared for the disorientation. She waited until the house was quiet, then turned the door handle.

In the next instant, three things happened at once.

First, a strong arm wrapped around her neck. Second, her phone dropped from her numb fingers. Third, she opened her mouth to scream.

A damp rag pressed over her mouth. She struggled, kicking and trying to bite the hand behind the rag. Cold liquid stung her nostrils, and she fought a sudden dizziness.

The rag moved away, and she took a breath to scream again, when the man shoved a handful of small, chalky items into her mouth. A hand clamped over her lips to keep her from spitting them out.

Fear heightened her strength, and she stamped her feet, trying to break his toes. The pills crushed against her teeth. The man wrenched her neck upward. She twisted her tongue away from the pills.

She gagged. Caught between two unpleasant choices, swallow or choke, her body made the choice for her, and she swallowed. She forced her limbs to relax, hoping he would think she had fainted. If he left, she could force herself to vomit.

Let go, damn it!

The man shifted his grip but did not move. Her mind swirled with fear until the world faded into shades of gray. She clung to consciousness, but it was a losing battle. With a final jerk of her limbs, she surrendered to darkness and slumped to the floor.

Chapter 11

Sebastian paced Chloe's basement for what felt like the hundredth time.

"I promise it is not as bad as you think, Peter," he said, rubbing his forehead with his thumb and middle finger. Were it anyone else, he would've sent them to voicemail. But Peter had been his friend for over a decade and was in the middle of a genuine crisis.

"I've called all her friends, but she's completely vanished," Peter said. There was a thread of hysteria in his usual calm voice. "Was it something I did? Do you think she figured out that I know she's seeing someone?"

You'd think someone died, the way he's going on.

He waited for Peter to stop babbling before answering. "Janet is probably just blowing off steam, trying to make you jealous."

"But what if she really is in trouble?"

He sighed. There was no point in telling Peter that if Janet hadn't taken any of her things with her, the odds were she would be back. Even if he convinced an officer at the station to put out a missing person's notice, nothing was going to be done until the morning. Half the streets in town were blocked by downed trees. The storm had been predicted to blow past them but at the last minute had changed course and hammered the small town.

"Keep trying her phone," Sebastian said instead. "If

you don't get an answer by tomorrow, I'll come help look for her. But honestly, Peter, this is classic Janet. Remember last time? You got into a huge panic, and then she showed up like nothing was wrong."

After that incident, he'd stopped trying to talk his friend into leaving Janet. As much as he loved to complain about her, Peter was utterly devoted to his wayward wife. It would take a truly heinous act—or a special woman—to keep him from chasing Janet to the ends of the earth.

"You're probably right," Peter said. "I swear, this is the last straw. I won't forgive her so easily if this really is a game."

That's exactly what you said last time.

He expected Peter to launch into a lengthy diatribe about Janet's failings and was prepared to cut him off when there was a shuffling upstairs. He muted his microphone, then looked up at the ceiling.

"Elena? Is that you?"

Another sound, like the squealing of furniture moving across the floor.

What is she doing up there, redecorating?

"Maybe I could just pop by the station," Peter said. "If something has happened to her, I'll never forgive myself."

Sebastian lowered his phone when he heard a scuffling, then a rhythmic pounding, like children jumping around. His chest tightened with worry. He unmuted his microphone and held it to his head. "I'm sorry, I have to go. I'll call you later."

He hung up before Peter could say anything else. Then he crept up the stairs to better hear what was going on. There was more thumping and scratching like someone was running their nails along the floor.

He flung the door open at the same time as thunder rumbled outside, and the lights flickered off. In the darkness, two figures struggled. One was Elena, the other a man in dark clothing. The man had pinned Elena's arms to her sides with one arm and with the other was shoving something into her mouth.

"Hey!" The words flew out of his mouth before he could claw them back.

The attacker spun around. He wore a balaclava that obscured his entire face except for small slits for his eyes and mouth.

Elena gave one last spasm, then went slack. The man slumped under the weight of her body, then released her. Her head hit the ground with a sick crunch.

The adrenaline coursing through Sebastian's body urged him to lash out, but he held back with an iron will. A second later, the attacker stepped away from Elena and pulled out a knife.

"Don't do this," Sebastian said, walking sideways so the man was forced to step away from Elena's prone body. He had to get to her, undo whatever her attacker had done. Blood spurted away from her head, following the grain of the wood on the floor. She was so still and slumped in an unnatural position.

Let her be okay. Please, God, I couldn't stand it if anything happened to her.

The man lunged, swiping his knife in an arc and narrowly missing Sebastian's face and cutting a slit in his shirt instead.

"What do you want?" Sebastian edged closer to Elena. "Money? My wallet is in the car outside." He pulled his keys from his pocket and threw them on the floor. "Take the car, too. But leave us alone."

The man took a step forward, raised his knife, then froze. He blinked several times, shook his head, then stumbled backward and ran out the front door. When it slammed shut, Sebastian fell to his knees and crawled over to Elena. He clasped her shoulders. She made a soft noise but didn't wake.

Not dead, at least.

But for how long?

****

Sebastian sped through another red light, fearing at any moment he would hear the wail of a police siren. In the back seat, Elena lay limp and broken like a discarded doll.

A silver hatchback cut him off, forcing him to slam on the brake. From the back seat, there was a low moan.

"Hang in there." He honked the horn. The hatchback braked, a finger coming up from the driver's side.

He tightened his hands on the wheel and swerved around the car. How much time had passed since he'd left the house? He wasn't sure. The clock on the dash wasn't working, and he couldn't risk pulling out his phone. Even if he did, he had no point of reference for when the drive had started. He felt as taut as a bow.

Elena moaned again and then lapsed into a coughing fit.

He glanced into the rear-view mirror to see her reaching out a hand and pointing to his head.

"What is it?" he darted his gaze between her hand and the road. "What's wrong?"

"S-sn-snake," she gurgled. "Tree. Shade. Shoulders."

She's losing it.

He clenched the wheel. She was drifting in and out of consciousness and not making sense.

A traffic light ahead flashed yellow, and Sebastian hit the gas, making his wheels squeal. Even the damn lights were against him. He screamed through the intersection.

In the back seat, Elena slid around the seats with every movement like a rag doll.

"Stay with me!"

He wasn't sure why it was so important for her to remain alert, but his gut told him if she fell asleep, she might never wake up again.

"Wake up!"

Her eyes fluttered open, then lowered again when he stopped talking.

If that's what it takes to keep you awake, I'll keep talking.

"You remember what Chloe was like, how she always took in strays?" Silence. With adrenaline rushing through his veins, each second passed like minutes.

A soft reply, "Jelly."

"Yes!" He sagged with relief. "The crow. I remember him. Do you remember how Chloe taught them? She had a way with animals. People kept telling her birds were untrainable." He paused, waiting for a response, fearing none would come.

I can't live without you. Please, God, don't die.

"T-teach anything w-with a brain."

He let out a heavy breath. "Yes, she always said that. She loved showing them off. Jump, play dead, fetch. She mastered them all. I think sometimes she spent more time with her animals than she did with us." He sailed past a stop sign, narrowly missing a sedan that swerved out of the way and wailed its horn. His entire body was a knot of tension.

"I saw Jelly," she whispered. Her words were growing softer. She was delirious. But there were only a few more blocks to go. They would make it.

They had to make it.

"I couldn't stand the way she lavished attention on them," Sebastian continued. "Those birds could do anything. She loved them more than she loved us." He couldn't stop the words pouring out of his mouth. "Remember how she used to get them to hide things for her?"

A whispered response, drowned out by the squeak of skin sliding against leather.

Sebastian ground his back teeth together.

The red lights of St. Augustine's Teaching Hospital appeared before him like the gates of heaven.

He remembered a town meeting years ago. Piled into the high school gymnasium, the only venue large enough to hold everyone, voting on a proposal to open a new hospital in Stillwood. He voted against it, insisting the local developers had bribed the town council to put forth the motion.

A significant number of wealthy business owners lived in Stillwood, seeking refuge from their hectic city lives. "Why should we send them into the city for their medical needs," the council argued. "When we can keep that money in the community?"

From the backseat, Elena groaned.

He reached back and squeezed her arm. Her skin was icy. "We're here. Hold on."

He pulled into the emergency entrance, took the keys out of the ignition, and jumped out of the car, waving at an older woman in scrubs who was smoking a cigarette around the corner from the ambulance loading dock.

He waved his arms. "I need help over here!"

The woman flicked her cigarette and jogged over to the car. He recognized her as the server from the diner, except her eyes were pools of black, and her teeth gleamed in the faint light. Then he blinked, and it wasn't a woman at all but a man wearing a name tag that read Ian Valencia.

"What's wrong?" Ian said.

Sebastian shook his head. "I need help. She hit her head."

Ian leaned into the car and looked at Elena. "She doesn't look good. I'll call for a stretcher."

Sebastian shoved him away, seeing something he hadn't noticed before. Blood was trickling out Elena's ear and dripping onto the seat.

A hot rush of fear hit him in the chest. Against Ian's protests, Sebastian gathered Elena into his arms and rushed into the emergency department. A sharp pain pierced his shoulder, and looked down to see Elena staring at him with wide, fearful eyes. She'd dug her nails into his arm.

"Don't let them possess me while I'm out," she said.

Startled by the intensity in her gaze, he nodded.

"Promise me!"

"I promise."

Her eyes flickered closed on a sigh.

A woman, he assumed she was a doctor from her white robe, took over, barking commands. "We don't have time for the usual intake," the doctor said. "Just give me the basics. Name? Age?"

"Elena Cain. Thirty-one."

"Any medical issues?"

He shifted, realizing how little he knew about her. "I don't know. Her mother didn't believe in traditional medicine."

"I see. Okay, just tell me what happened leading up to the event."

He explained what he'd seen, anxiety growing with each passing minute. He finished, and the doctor led him to the waiting room. "Wait here. We'll call you when you can see her."

The hospital staff left, and Sebastian fell into a chair. The energy that had sustained him throughout the drive drained away. Like a recording, the scene repeated in his head. Elena crumpled on the floor. Cut. Lifting her up, shaking her limp frame. Cut. Out the door, placing her unresponsive body in the back seat. Repeat.

He tried to banish the image of Elena from his mind. Each time he thought he'd succeeded, she returned, eyes blazing with accusation, face contorted with rage.

You should have saved me, she said. *You should have saved us both.*

He buried his face in his hands until the sounds around him faded away.

****

"You can see her now."

The sound of paper shuffling. "Mr. Castillo?"

Sebastian jerked awake at the touch of a hand on his shoulder. A woman stood in front of him, wearing turquoise scrubs. Her hair was pulled back into a high ponytail, and she held a clipboard. Behind her, doctors rushed to and from the nurses' station, the stethoscopes around their necks bouncing.

Sebastian rubbed the grit from his eyes. "Sorry, what did you say?"

The woman seized his wrist. "Wash your hands before you do that." She stepped back. "Your wife is awake. Come with me."

"She's not my—" Sebastian started, but the nurse was already walking away.

I guess it's fine if they think we're married.

They walked through a set of double-hinged doors that clanked open and closed, then down a long hall. His hands shook as they passed rooms full of patients hooked up to machines until, at last, they stopped.

"She's in here," the woman said. She placed her clipboard in a plastic container on the wall. "Visiting hours end at six." Then she spun on her heel and marched back down the hall, her ponytail bobbing with each step.

Sebastian stared at the closed door, his heart pounding in his ears. He sanitized his hands using the dispenser near the bathroom, then took a long drink of water from the fountain a few feet away.

It's just a hospital. People come and go all the time. It's fine.

He pushed the door open.

For a fleeting moment, the space held the echo of a different hospital room. A pale boy lay there, connected by a plethora of tubes to a wall of gently whirring machines. The boy's eyes shot open, and he removed the mask from his face with a shaking hand.

"Where were you?" Edward asked. "I waited for you. Why didn't you come?"

Reality swam into focus. It was Elena, not Edward. It was the present, and he'd made it in time. She would not die alone, abandoned by someone she trusted. He shook off the chains of his past and sat by the bed.

The sight of her pained him. Her inky hair was fanned around the small pillow, and her face was relaxed in slumber. She looked innocent. Fragile. He could not believe he was applying those words to Elena Cain. She'd always been so strong.

He remembered the day Chloe had dared her to climb the old maple tree in their backyard. The look of disgust on Elena's face made them both laugh. She marched them outside and scrambled up the tree like a monkey, then hooted and hollered at them from the uppermost branches while swinging upside down by her knees. Then Elena's mother spotted them from her kitchen window and screamed. Chloe and Sebastian laughed until they were blue in the face. They'd all gotten grounded for that charade.

How long would it be before his memory of Chloe faded? Before he forgot the sound of her voice?

"I miss it," he said out loud. "How the three of us were back then. Before life tore us apart."

He blamed himself for her departure. After Edward died, he lost all concept of self. The only thing that mattered was bringing his brother's killer to justice. By the time he came out of that fugue, it was too late.

He took one of her thin hands and recoiled. She was as cold as death.

He rummaged around the room until he found a blanket in a plastic container in the closet. Gently, so as not to wake her, he tucked her limbs beneath the blanket and folded the ends under her body. She looked like an ancient Egyptian corpse being prepared for burial, but at least she'd be warm.

He thumped down into the nearest chair and gently

scooted it closer, remembering the man he'd fought. Had it been the killer? If so, what had he been doing in Chloe's house—looking for the hard drive?

Or maybe he was after Elena.

He stilled. Had she seen something when she'd arrived at the house? Was that why the killer had come after her?

"Bast," Elena whispered.

He crowded closer. "I'm here."

Her head rocked back and forth, eyes moving beneath her eyelids. He smoothed her hair out of her face. "Shh, it's okay. I won't leave."

She settled, and as Sebastian looked down on her smiling face, affection bubbled up and consumed him. Despite everything they had been through and how painful it had to be for her with reminders of her past everywhere, she had stayed with him

He brushed his lips against her cheek, breathed in the gentle scent of minty shampoo that clung to her hair, and whispered the words that burned in his heart.

"I love you."

Chapter 12

Elena awoke to blindingly bright light. She was in a bed, surrounded by a plasticky curtain. There was a mix of muted voices interrupted by the clattering of wheels. The chilled air settled in her lungs and made her cough.

Where am I?

"Elena?"

A blurred face appeared. She tried to respond, but her body wouldn't obey. Tendrils coiled around her consciousness and drowned her in smothering darkness. Meanwhile, her hand touched Sebastian's cheek.

He kissed her fingers. "I'm so glad you're awake."

No, that's not me!

She pushed against her restraints, but they held firm. It was exactly as she'd feared. In her weakened state, a shade had slipped past her barriers and taken possession of her body.

What did that mean? Was she changing somehow, becoming more susceptible to the shade's influence? Was she on the brink of succumbing, like her mother before her?

Sebastian, run! Get away from me!

She had a flashback of her mother leaning over Edward's prone body, a bloody knife held above her head.

No!

If the shade hurt Sebastian, then the moment she got

free, she would track it down by whatever means necessary. She'd never destroyed a shade before, but she'd find a way.

But the shade didn't rise or lash out. Instead, it squeezed Sebastian's fingers. The action was accompanied by a gentle brush of concern against her mind. It was so unlike what she'd expected that she recoiled.

"I've missed you, Bast," the shade said. "You have no idea how much. But you have to stop him."

Stop who? The killer?

She reached for the presence sharing her body and was swept into a memory.

She was on a moving swing, pumping her legs back and forth. Adrenaline rushed to her stomach and made her giggle. Then she leaped from the swing in an arc and landed with her feet together and her arms raised in a Y position.

"Ta-da!" she cried. Then she looked at Sebastian, leaning against a large elm tree. "What do you think? Roth says I should try out for the cheerleading team."

"I don't know what you see in him," Sebastian said. His arms were folded over his chest, and the muscles in his neck stood out as if he was physically holding himself back from throttling her.

"He's nice, okay?" Chloe said, even though she didn't expect Sebastian to understand. Roth made her feel things she'd never felt before, and in a small town where she'd known everyone since she could toddle, the newness of it was exciting.

"He's a bastard," Sebastian snarled. "I saw the bruises on your arms last night. I know what he did to you."

She plucked at the cuffs of her sweater with her fingers. "That was an accident."

They'd been at Roth's apartment, and she'd accidentally broken a dish he'd inherited from his mother. Of course, he got mad. But he cried and held her after, insisting it was a mistake. Roth would never hurt her.

Would he?

As the memory faded, Elena realized two things.

First, the shade that had been possessing her was indeed Chloe. Second, Detective Roth was a viable suspect. Even though Chloe's memory of that incident was filled with happiness, there was a tinge of doubt in her heart. Combined with the earlier memory she'd gleaned from Roth, she was more suspicious than ever.

She shook off the memory and concentrated on what the shade was doing with her body. It might have been Chloe once, but that didn't make it any less dangerous. She tensed and waited for the right moment to strike.

Sebastian frowned. "Are you okay? You're not making sense again." He placed his palm on her forehead, then shook his head and pulled his arm back. "Your fever seems to have passed, at least."

The shade sighed, and its sorrow wreathed around Elena, squeezing her tight. "I have to go now," it said. "I'll talk to you later, I hope."

The pressure in Elena's head vanished, and she popped back into her own body.

"Where are you going?" Sebastian smiled. It was clear from his expression that he thought she was still loopy from the drugs or whatever else she'd been subjected to.

"N-nowhere," Elena started. Then her stomach

squeezed, and there was a sour tang in the back of her throat. She retched, and Sebastian shoved a plastic tub into her arms. She gripped the bowl, panting as bile churned in her stomach. When the nausea finally passed, she downed the water Sebastian handed her and scraped the metallic taste off her tongue with her teeth. A thick substance filled her mouth. She spat a mass of green phlegm into the tub.

"Here," Sebastian said, holding out a box of tissues. She accepted it with a croaked thanks, then blew her nose until her ears popped.

"All good?" Sebastian took the tissue box. The concern written in the wrinkles around his eyes sent butterflies flying in her stomach.

"I think so," she said. Her voice was still rough, but the rattling in her chest had stopped. "Where am I? What happened?"

"St. Augustine's. The doctors said if I hadn't—" His already pale face blanched. "It doesn't matter." Then he raised her hand to his lips and kissed the center of her palm. "You're safe now."

The python wrapped around his neck uncoiled and disappeared beneath his collar. A second later, it traveled along his arm and through their connected hands to her forearm, then vanished beneath her hospital gown.

Hello, there.

She reached for the shade's presence in her mind, instinctually knowing it had no intention of possessing her.

Who are you, anyway?

There was a fizzing that sounded almost like laughter, but it was over so quickly she dismissed it as background hospital noise.

That's when a fact, overlooked, sprang to the surface of her mind. Sebastian's face was dark with growth as if he hadn't shaved in days. The window behind him was bright, and the clock on the wall revealed it was early morning.

Although she dreaded the answer, she asked, "How long have I been out?"

He stared at her.

Her chest rattled again and sent her into a coughing fit. Sebastian pounded on her back to dispel the mucous. The python coiled around Sebastian's neck.

"Two days," Sebastian said.

Her mind reeled. How was that possible? If she'd been out for so long, surely a shade would have taken over her body and caused chaos?

Unless whatever drugs the hospital had given her had interfered with the process. That would explain why she'd only been possessed once she awoke.

She filed away that information for later analysis. She'd never considered the possibility of using drugs to keep the shades at bay.

Sebastian crowded her as she propped herself up. She shoved his hands away. "Stop fussing! I'm fine." She wound back her memory, but it was fuzzy and hard to grasp. "I remember Sandra picked the lock at Chloe's house. Then what happened?"

He studied her face. "I went into the basement to answer a call and left you upstairs. The call took longer than I thought. Then I heard sounds and came upstairs to find you being attacked by a masked man."

She touched her lips, remembering how the man had jerked her head upright. "He shoved something in my mouth. Pills, I think."

Was that why they'd kept her in the hospital for so long? Had it been the pills that had knocked her out, not anything the doctors had given her?

There was also the terrible pounding in her head.

Sebastian's shoulders slumped. "I'm sorry. It's my fault. I left you there. I failed you."

Elena shot her arm out from under the protective covering of the blanket to punch his shoulder. "Stop that. It's fine. I'm fine. I don't enjoy knowing my attacker is walking the streets, but…"

A damp rag pressed over her mouth. Arms closed around her, pulling her from the closet. She struggled, kicking and trying to bite the hand behind the rag.

Darkness crept in from the edges of her vision.

Beep, beep, beep.

A nurse in turquoise scrubs shoved aside the curtain with a crinkling sound. Her shock-white hair was tied in a high ponytail, and her eyes were pools of black. She smiled, revealing a mouthful of sharp teeth.

Elena was about to scream, but when the nurse stepped inside, her white hair warmed to a golden brown, and the teeth that had been razor sharp were lined with metal brackets.

"Visiting hours are over," the nurse said, the braces giving her a slight lisp. "Family only."

"No!" Elena cried.

The sterile environment was little more than another kind of cage, one she couldn't escape on her own. If Sebastian left, she'd be at their mercy. Visions of needles, whirring machines, and flashing lights filled her mind.

"I'm family," he said to the nurse. "Her husband."

My what?

"Sorry about that," he whispered after the nurse had left. "They just assumed."

"It's fine," she said. "Can you get me more water?" Her throat was parched.

After Sebastian exited the room, she moved her arms and legs. Nothing hurt, aside from the needle in her wrist. She raised her other arm and probed her scalp, touching something tender. Her head throbbed. The room spun. "Crap. Crap." She took steady, deep breaths until her nausea passed.

Sebastian returned, and when he looked at her, he frowned and stepped closer. "You don't look so great."

"Speak for yourself. You look like shit."

Sebastian unwound enough to laugh. Then his face became serious. "As much as I don't want to talk to Roth, we should report this."

Elena scoffed. "Why? He didn't believe us the last time."

They looked at each other for a long moment, smiles fading. There were bags under his eyes, and his hair stuck up at odd angles.

"You've been here the whole time," she said.

Sebastian winced but didn't correct her.

"Damn. We're back to square one. Well, what happened while I was out?"

Sebastian shifted in his chair. "The coroner released his report. The official cause of death is accidental drowning."

Elena slammed her head back on the pillow. Each new snippet of information she gathered was a piece of the larger puzzle, one she could not yet recognize. But when she looked around her small room, she shuddered. One thing was certain.

"I can't stay here."

"They'll discharge you now that you're awake."

Elena couldn't tell if he misunderstood or if the thought of her leaving town was too painful for him to grasp. She remembered a time years ago when they'd had a similar argument. She had begged her parents for months for permission to attend a summer camp. Perhaps because she hadn't yet developed her talents, her mother relented and signed the form allowing her to go. When she showed the paper to Sebastian, his face developed the same stony expression. For a kid, three months was forever. Elena longed for freedom to stretch her wings, but Sebastian refused to accept her logic, closing her out of his life and giving her the silent treatment. It was too much for her, as young and vulnerable as she was, and with few friends outside of the Castillo family. She begged forgiveness and promised she would never leave again.

She lifted herself into a sitting position. "I want to find out what happened to Chloe as much as you do, but it's getting too dangerous."

Sebastian crossed his arms. "You can't leave. Someone tried to kill you. How do we know they won't just follow you?"

He didn't understand, couldn't understand.

All it would take is one moment of weakness. One moment, and the right shade, and he's dead.

A shade didn't need a knife to kill him. She might be physically weaker than Sebastian, but there were far too many ways to kill, and she couldn't count on him to fight back.

"You can't keep running forever," Sebastian said. "Why not let me help you?"

Elena sighed. "What if the killer comes after me again and you get hurt? I can't take that risk. It's better if I run."

It wouldn't be anything new. She'd run for so long that staying in one place felt wrong. The longest she'd slept in the same bed since leaving her aunt's had been measured in weeks, not months.

Sebastian ran a hand through his hair, further messing it up. "Why are you keeping me out? We were like siblings, once."

Elena snorted. "Really? What kind of siblings sneak out of their houses at midnight to make out in the forest?" Hardening her heart, she reminded herself of the stakes. Her life was her own to bet, but she wouldn't risk his.

Sebastian buried his face in his hands, his elbows on his knees. "You don't understand how difficult this is for me."

Guilt hit her like a punch in the gut. She wrapped her arms around his neck, drawing him close. "You were there, weren't you, when Edward died in the hospital?"

Sebastian sniffed. "I was in detention, so I didn't know until they called. The school told me that much, but I told myself it was a minor injury, that he'd be out of the hospital in a few days." Sebastian took a long breath. "I got there too late. Edward was already dead."

"I'm sorry."

"When I saw you on the floor at Chloe's, all I could think was, please don't let it happen again. I couldn't bear to see anything happen to you."

She pulled his head into her chest and nuzzled his hair. He smelled terrible, like sweat and stale beer, but at that moment, she would've given anything to keep holding him forever.

Then the curtain around the bed slid to the side, and they sprang apart. A tall Black man with close-cropped hair and the white robe of a doctor walked in. He checked the machines around the bed and then looked at them. "Hello, Elena. How are you feeling?"

"My head hurts."

The doctor picked up the clipboard at the bottom of the bed, studied it, then laughed. "Yes, I expect it would!"

She clenched her hands. "Why? What happened to me?"

The doctor flipped through the paperwork on the sheet. "You scared the nurses half to death."

Elena squeezed her fingers around Sebastian's. "Why? What did you find?"

The doctor took a plastic bag out of his pocket and handed it to Sebastian, who opened it and withdrew a small green square.

"It feels hard, like metal," Sebastian said. He held out his hand for Elena to see. She craned her neck. It was green and black with small lumps of silver. "What the hell is that?"

"I'm not sure. It was embedded in your scalp. When we took you in for an MRI, it ripped right out."

Elena stared at the chip, then touched the back of her head. "You're serious? That thing was inside me?"

Had someone injected it into her? When could that have happened? Delicate shivers raced down her limbs. Someone had violated her, implanted a device inside her. It was not a pleasant feeling.

"Where did it come from?" Sebastian held the piece with his thumb and index finger.

The doctor flipped another few pages on her chart.

"We assumed you knew. There were old surgery scars on Elena's head. Someone put it in there."

Elena looked at Sebastian and knew he was thinking the same thing. They had a tech genius to visit.

****

Getting out of the hospital was easier said than done.

The doctors insisted she submit to further tests, saying that leaving without knowing why she'd lapsed into a coma for so long was dangerous. She set her jaw and repeated the word "no" until someone gave her a form to sign.

Still, she didn't grasp the truth of how close she'd come to death until she saw the interior of Sebastian's car. It was splattered with blood, and the seats and carpet gave off a metallic, bitter smell that assaulted her senses.

Someone tried to kill me. And they almost succeeded.

"I'll pay for you to have this taken care of," she said, voice tight. She didn't have the money, but she'd find a way.

Sebastian shrugged. "It's fine. I have a friend who owns a detailing shop who owes me a favor."

"Thank you."

He glanced at her. "For what?"

"Getting me to the hospital. Saving my life."

Sebastian smiled. The same smile that had entranced her as a teenager. She turned away. It would be so much easier to pretend everything was normal. If only that was possible.

You're going to get him killed next.

She considered the facts. Someone wanted her out of town. That was clear from the goggles and the phone call. In any other situation, she would've chalked it up to the Harvester, but subtle games didn't match his pattern. He was a more "in-your-face" kind of monster. Even the attack at Chloe's house felt off, like it was a crime of opportunity.

Then there were Chloe's messages. First, she'd drawn the word *help* on the mirror. That one was easy to understand. She wanted them to find her murderer. Then the words *find research stop him*. The last two words were obvious, and the "him" had to be the killer, confirming it was a male. Not that it was surprising. She'd already gleaned as much from Chloe's last memory.

But what did "find research" mean? What research?

An idea wormed its way through her mind.

"Do you remember the scavenger hunts?"

He gave her an appraising glance. "Why?"

"She was always very good at hiding things. But not very good at giving clues."

The car fell silent again.

Before Elena knew it, they were pulling into Sandra's building.

When they were in the elevator, he crossed his arms. "So, you think she hid something for us to find?"

"Exactly. We just have to find whatever it is. I'm sure that's what Chloe wants. I mean, what she would have wanted."

Sebastian's lips thinned, but he nodded.

They knocked on Sandra's door, and when she opened it, Elena pulled the bag with the microchip from in her pocket and held it up.

Sandra reached out, and when their hands touched, an arc of electricity sparked. Elena dropped the bag.

"Sorry about that," Sandra said, catching the bag

mid-air. "Occupational hazard." She lifted the bag and frowned. "Where did you get this?"

Elena exchanged glances with Sebastian, who gave a slight nod.

"It was in my head," she said.

Sandra's eyebrows rose. "Really?"

Elena pointed to the chip. "It's some kind of computer chip, right?"

Sandra snorted. "A little more sophisticated, but you're on the right track. I've seen this before. Farmers implant similar devices into their cattle to stop them from wandering away. Someone's been monitoring you."

Elena's world slanted on its axis. Someone had been tracking her, following her. The violation made the acid roil in her stomach and left her with a clammy feeling like she'd just crawled out of an ice-cold bath. An image of herself as a cow flashed into her mind. In that scenario, the killer was a wolf lurking around the edges of her pasture.

"What kind of range does that thing have?" Sebastian asked.

Sandra set the chip down. "Depends on the reader and the chip. Anywhere from a few inches to 25 feet. I'll know more when I take this one apart."

That made her feel better but was still unsettling.

"The doctors said there was an old surgical scar," Elena said. "Which means someone put that thing in my head. Do you have any clue how long it might have been there?"

Sandra examined the chip. "We-ell, this isn't new. They can make them the size of a grain of rice now. I'd say it's almost twenty years old."

Elena's knees wobbled. "Oh, no."

The other occupants of the room stared at her. When she didn't speak up, Sebastian nudged her with his knee. "Care to share with the class?"

She rested her elbows on her knees. "After I left Stillwood, I stayed with my aunt. There was an incident. I broke my arm, and they took me to the hospital. I thought I would just get a cast and then come right home, but they knocked me out, saying it would be too painful. When I woke up, my head was sore."

She remembered that day vividly because Aunt Martha had been acting strangely, and she had caught on to it. At the time, she'd thought her aunt was worried for her sake and had reassured her it was a simple break. Nothing to worry about.

Sandra dropped the chip onto a glass plate with a chink. "Parents. These days they track their kids' phones with apps."

Elena looked at the chip and tried not to let the throbbing in her head translate to tears. The image of her mother in her mind was shattered.

"Don't let this get to you," Sandra said. She pulled Elena into a tight embrace. "It's not your fault. Parents aren't perfect. They make mistakes, too."

Elena tolerated the physical contact for a minute before pulling away. The Persian had returned to Sandra's cheek and was grooming its fur.

"Leave the chip with me," Sandra said. "If there's anything more to find, I'll find it."

Chapter 13

When they returned to the condo, Elena accepted Sebastian's offer of a stiff drink, then crossed the shag carpet to flop on the leather sofa.

How did I get involved in this?

She had only intended to come to Stillwood to sell the house and had somehow been roped into investigating a murder.

Sebastian turned on the TV to the local news, lowered the volume, then joined her on the couch with two glasses of amber liquid. He stayed a respectable distance away, which both pleased and chafed her. After fighting the urge for far too long, she shifted closer so their thighs touched.

A smile flitted across his face. She leaned her head against his shoulder, and he wrapped an arm around her.

"We'll figure this out," she whispered.

His exhale ruffled her hair. "I know. I just wish you hadn't gotten involved. Maybe then—"

"I've been through worse," she interrupted, squeezing his thigh. "Trust me."

Something soft brushed her hand. It was Silky, sticking her nose into the glass of whiskey. She downed the alcohol and then set the glass on the counter. "You got the cats?"

Sebastian kneeled and rubbed the Tiger's head. "I would not let them go to the pound. They're family.

Though I didn't know she had two. I've never met the orange one."

"I call him Tiger," she said, reaching down to touch the cat. He jumped out of her way, then hissed. The white tip of his tail swished back and forth along the carpet.

"They're temperamental," Sebastian said. "Don't worry, they'll get used to you."

Silky peeked at her from behind the TV stand. Elena rubbed her fingers together. The cat ran away.

She loved cats, but they never took to her.

"I told you," Sebastian said with a laugh.

Tiger flopped over on his side, exposing an extremely fluffy white tummy.

She ran her fingers through the soft fur. Then Silky startled her by jumping onto her lap and dropping something from her mouth.

"Hello, sweetie. What did you bring me?" She fetched the object from where it had slid between the cushions. An orange ball.

She stroked the cat's soft fur. "What's this for, huh?" She raised the ball, and Silky's eyes followed it. "Where did you get this?"

Sebastian pointed to cardboard box in a corner. "It took them less than an hour to break into it and rip the catnip bag apart."

Crafty buggers.

She palmed the toy, and it rattled. She inspected the ball and found small holes along its surface.

"Oh, no wonder you love this." She popped open the latch and confirmed it was filled with treats. She dropped the ball, and Silky chased after it, batting it around the room before taking it into her mouth and returning to the couch, holding the large ball off the ground with her head in the air. Elena laughed with delight. "You can fetch!"

"Chloe probably trained them," Sebastian said.

They looked at the box of toys in unison.

The perfect place to hide something you don't want found.

Sebastian retrieved the box and put it on the coffee table. Toy after toy clattered to the ground, but there was no trace of a micro-SD card.

Damn.

Then Tiger padded closer, a deep purr reverberating from his throat.

"Come here, sweetie," she cooed, rubbing her fingers together. Tiger stepped right over her and butted his head against Sebastian's face.

Double damn.

"Why do they never love me as much as I love them?"

"Gotta play hard to get," Sebastian said, extracting Tiger's claws from his shirt. "They can sense neediness a mile away. Here, let me try something." He pulled a large blanket over top of them, wrapped an arm around her shoulders, and spread the blanket over their laps. Tiger obligingly jumped up and stretched out, and Silky followed soon after.

"Genius move," she whispered. She fished through the blanket and found his hand, and then squeezed it. Then she turned her head and pressed her lips against his. The chaste peck deepened, and heat pooled between her thighs. Excitement thrilled along her nerves and raised the tiny hairs along her arms.

The cats scrambled off them, and they rose and stumbled into Sebastian's bedroom. She focused on the feel of his mouth against hers, the seductive movement of his tongue. A premonition of what would happen next flickered through her mind and heightened her arousal. He broke from her mouth and trailed hot, open-mouthed kisses along her neck that sent pleasure coursing through her veins.

She shrugged off her clothes. A shushing noise told her Sebastian was doing the same.

"Wow."

She smiled. "Like what you see?"

Sebastian ran a hand along her thigh. "You are beautiful."

"Less looking, more kissing."

Soon they were laying on the bed, and the hot, rigid length of him pressed against her stomach. She wiggled her hips and elicited a low moan.

He grasped her bottom in his hands and anchored her in place. "Quit that, you minx." He pushed aside her hair to whorl his tongue in the space where her neck met her shoulder. The sensation curled her toes, and she tilted her head to give him better access.

"Oh, oh yes. Right there. Keep doing that." He rasped his tongue up her neck, nipping and sucking. His hand left her ass, and she was about to complain when he brought the hand back in a spank that shocked through her like electricity and startled a gasp from her lips.

He chuckled and kneaded her sore bottom. "Like that, did you?" He took her earlobe into his mouth and bit down. "Do you want more?"

"No," she replied, smiling. "It's my turn. Protection?"

He jerked his head toward the table. She searched the drawer and took out a strawberry-flavored condom. She unwrapped it, found the correct orientation, and with the condom inside her mouth, leaned forward and unrolled it over the rigid length of him until he pressed against the back of her throat. One hand pushed the rest of the contraceptive down to the base of his shaft. She closed her lips and sucked, smiling as he uttered a curse and threaded his hands through her hair.

"Oh, God, Elena." He panted and squeezed his fingers against her scalp.

She held his hips down and continued to lavish attention on his cock, increasing the pressure as he grew thicker in her mouth. The feeling of him was fascinating, silky smooth and rock hard at the same time.

****

She was alive against him, a writhing siren of a woman calling forth carnal desires he had thought long dead. As her mouth worked, he struggled to keep an iron grip on his passion, keeping himself right on the edge of climax without falling over. When he could bear it no longer, he lifted her head and looked into passion-filled eyes that tightened something in his chest.

"I'd like to come while inside you," he said.

Elena's lips parted, and she nodded. She crawled on top of him and, with excruciating slowness, guided him to her entrance, coating him in her essence. The motion sent shocks of pleasure through him, and he had to resist the urge to thrust before she was ready.

"You're killing me," he said, clenching his hands in the sheets.

After a lifetime of tortuous sliding, her lips pressed around him. He forced himself to stay still and moaned as she lowered herself down, her velvet folds clamping around him like a vice. She was so tight he feared he might hurt her if he moved too fast, so he let her set the rhythm until she grabbed his hands and placed them on her hips.

"Guide me," she said. Then she held up a small vibrator he kept in the side table. "I hope you don't mind if I use this."

Sebastian took over, pushing her hips up and down, increasing the speed of their joining and allowing his climax to build. He jerked the moment she put the vibrator to her most sensitive area. Then he slowed and thrust deeper, noticing she preferred him deep and slow rather than shallow and fast.

A few minutes later, she climaxed. He stilled, waiting for her to relax, then thrust twice and joined her.

****

Elena cuddled closer to the warm expanse of man and had a flash of self-consciousness. Once the shudders stopped, she grabbed the vibrator from where it fell and turned it back on.

"Thanks for letting me use this," she wiggled the vibrator. "If you don't mind me using it again, I always orgasm in threes."

He chuckled, and she murmured her appreciation as firm hands ran up her thighs. His fingers flicked against her entrance, then slipped away.

"Can I help?" he asked.

"Oh, yes, please," she said as her second orgasm spiraled closer.

Fingers speared through her, curling upward and sending waves of pleasure from her pelvis and up her chest. Seconds later, her orgasm hit and shocked her with its intensity, rippling down from the tip of her head to her toes.

His fingers slowed, then stopped, but remained

inside her. Once her shudders stilled, he guided her to a third orgasm that rolled over her in bursts of heat.

Spent, she dropped the vibrator. Sebastian raised his fingers to his lips and sucked the remains of her essence from them. He settled against her back, one arm wrapped around her middle until his warmth seeped into her bones.

****

Elena lay in the bed, cuddled in layers of thick blankets. Sebastian snored beside her with one arm splayed over her hip.

I wish we could stay like this forever.

Being with him was everything she'd wished for, and more. He was kind, sensitive, and protective without being possessive.

He deserves better.

Her chest itched, and she absently scratched with one hand. The itching got worse, and she peeled the blankets away to see the boa staring up at her from between her breasts.

"What?" she whispered. "Do you actually want to help, for once?"

The boa flicked its tongue, and the itchiness on her chest crept up her neck until she had to crush her hands beneath her back to keep from scratching like a flea-ridden stray. She wasn't surprised when the pressure came, starting in her throat like she'd swallowed a water balloon.

She searched out the boa in her mind. The spark was there but dim. She tried to connect to it but received only gentle whispers in response. She closed her eyes and reached for the spark again.

Images bloomed into her mind, one after another in

layers, faded and watery like the reflection in a pond. Too fast to follow. She grasped Chloe's essence and wrapped her in a warm embrace, soothing the swirling mass of energy.

The images slowed, transparent and hard to grasp, but if she focused, she could make them out.

No, a voice whispered in her mind. *Don't fight it. Let me in.*

For once, she didn't resist, and instead of being held by invisible bonds in the darkness of her mind, the shade slipped in beside her. She experimentally wiggled her fingers and toes, confirming she hadn't lost control. Rather than being ousted, it felt more like someone was sharing her mind with her.

Hello, Chloe's voice whispered in her head. *I was wondering how long it would take you to figure it out. You were always so stubborn, Ellie.*

Elena's eyes burned with tears, and her throat worked.

"I'm so sorry, Chloe," she whispered. "If I had gotten there sooner, you might not have—"

Enough of that, Chloe interrupted. *As cool as it is being dead, I'd really like to move on. Edward says the afterlife is amazing.*

Her heart skipped a beat. "Edward?"

He insists on staying with Sebastian until this is all over.

The python. Of course. The memories she'd received from it were of his time in the hospital.

We don't have long, Chloe said. *I can't maintain this forever.*

"Of course. I understand. You want us to find who killed you, right?"

A swell of anger made her skin flush.

Sorry, Chloe said. *This sharing thing is weird. Yes, find him and stop him before he kills again. He won't stop. He can't.*

Elena had read enough about serial killers to understand, but even if she hadn't, she'd experienced their memories. She knew the compulsion to kill, the addiction. It was irresistible.

"Who is it?"

I don't know. Ugh. I keep trying to remember, but the memories are hazy. I remember it was a man, and that it was someone I knew, but that's all.

No more than Elena had already surmised from experiencing Chloe's memories herself. Not that she'd expected anything else. That would've been too easy.

One more thing. Chloe paused. *You won't like it.*

"Just tell me," Elena said with a sigh. "I'm already neck-deep in trouble."

Muted laughter, then Chloe's voice again, more serious this time. *Tell my brother everything.*

"What!"

Elena slapped a hand over her mouth.

Sebastian murmured and shifted, turning away from her.

I said you wouldn't like it. But he has to know. It's not safe keeping him in the dark.

Chloe's words twisted her up inside, but her friend had a point. Telling Sebastian about the real enemy they faced gave him a fighting chance.

"Okay." She swallowed the moisture in her mouth. "I'll tell him as soon as he wakes up."

Thanks, Ellie. You're the best.

With a sound like air escaping from a balloon, the

other consciousness in her mind drifted away. Then Sebastian rolled to face her. "Who were you talking to?"

"No one," Elena said before remembering what she'd promised Chloe. It was instinctual to always protect herself. Then she glanced down. The boa curled above her breasts, tongue flicking in and out. She took a deep breath to calm her racing heart.

You have to tell him.

Sebastian wrapped his arm around her waist. "You know you can tell me what's bothering you, right? You don't have to hide things from me."

She pressed her ear to his chest to hear the even thump of his heart. "I know. I'm just scared."

His palm stroked down her back. "Scared of what?"

"Scared you won't believe me."

He kissed her neck. "Whatever it is, we'll deal with it together. Trust me."

Elena blew out a breath. "Okay."

****

Sebastian waited in the kitchen, preparing himself for the worst.

A thousand scenarios flitted through his mind. The most prominent of those was that Elena had a mental illness, such as schizophrenia. Such things were hereditary, or at least ran in families. And there was no doubt Elena's mother had been ill.

It doesn't matter. She's still Elena. Whatever it is, we'll deal with it.

Even if that meant doctor's visits, time in treatment centers. It didn't matter. He'd stay by her side, come what may.

But when Elena sat beside him, he realized he hadn't prepared enough.

"I was talking to a shade," she said. "They're like moving tattoos. I can see them on my skin and on others."

He stared at her, speechless.

She laughed nervously. "They used to be living people like you and me."

"You mean ghosts?"

"Pretty much, yeah."

He was silent again, then frowned, "You see them all the time?"

"Yes."

"How long have you—"

"Since I was a kid."

He shook his head. "I can't imagine what it's like."

"It's like being in Vegas. Moving advertisements and billboards everywhere. It's overwhelming. But you get used to it."

She thinks she can see ghosts.

It was worse than he'd thought.

He sighed. "You're not well, Elena."

"I knew you couldn't handle the truth," she said. Her shoulders drooped, and he cursed himself. This was the girl he'd skipped stones with and kissed under a full winter moon. The girl who braided Chloe's hair and helped them build a snow fort every winter. He had to give her a chance, no matter how incredible her story sounded.

"You understand why I'm having a hard time believing this," he said.

She sniffed. "This is why I didn't want to stay with you. I'm not normal."

"I'm sorry," he said and meant it. He watched the play of emotion across her face. "Chloe," he said, finally.

"That's who you think you were talking to."

"Yes." She rubbed her hands together. "I didn't know she could talk to me, not until today."

His heart ached at the thought of his sister sticking around like a guardian angel. Then he mentally shook himself. Ghosts weren't real. Elena could believe whatever she wanted, but he would not encourage her.

"I guess I'll have to show you," she said. Her eyes rolled back in her head. Her skin paled until it was almost transparent. He shook her. "Stop this, come back!"

Her head lolled to the side, and he only just caught her as she crumpled. He laid her on the floor, cupping her neck with his hand and willing her to move until her eyelashes fluttered open.

"What was that?" he whispered. "What happened?"

She pushed his arms away. "Jeese, you really are dense."

An ice-cold electric current shot through him. The voice was different from Elena's, pitched higher.

"C-Chloe? Is that you?"

She rolled her eyes. "Who else would it be, dummy?"

Sebastian pulled his sister into his arms against her snarling protests. He rose and twirled her around three times before setting her down.

"What happened to Elena?"

Chloe wrinkled her nose. "She's still here, listening. She let me in, but I don't think she knows how to kick me out."

Sebastian squeezed his sister once more, ignoring her feeble attempts to push him away. "God, Chloe. I thought I'd never talk to you again."

"Jesus, Bast, I get it. Can you let me go before you

crush the rest of the bones in this body?"

With a significant force of will, he let her go. She settled on the other side of the couch, crossing her legs and pushing the hair out of her face before leveling him with an even stare. It felt so wrong, like Elena was doing a disturbingly accurate impression of his sister. He flopped into a chair.

"This feels so strange," Chloe said, twisting her wrists around and around. "It's like I'm wearing her as a costume. I can move her body, but it doesn't obey me perfectly." She picked up her shirt away from her chest and looked down. "But it's better than being a snake."

"You remember that?" What else could she remember?

"Bits and pieces," Chloe said. She ran her palms down her thighs. "Elena still has a terrible sense of style, I see."

Sebastian clenched his hands and almost laughed at the familiar jolt of frustration. Chloe had a way of getting under his skin. Siblings were like that. He pushed away his emotions and asked the most important question.

"Do you remember who killed you?"

She folded her hands in her lap and looked at them. "My memories are foggy. I know I was at the Cain house, but that's all." Chloe jerked her head up, her eyes wide. "I can hear Elena's voice. She's telling me it's normal because of trauma."

Sebastian sighed. "I guess it was too much to hope it would be that easy. What do you remember?"

"I remember doing research. I wanted to know what really happened to Edward." She shot him a glare. "Because you refused to listen. I found out something. What was it?" She slammed her hands on the couch. "I can't remember!"

She looked so anguished. He slid closer and wrapped an arm around her shoulders. "Hey, it's okay, don't worry. We'll figure this out."

She shrugged off his embrace. "I hid something. I remember that. Something important. My research." She clutched her head and whined. "This hurts, Bast. Everything hurts."

"You can rest soon, I promise," he soothed. "But we have to know so we can find your killer. Think, sis. Where is it?"

She scrunched up her face. "I think I left it with an animal. A bird? There were sticks. A lot of sticks. And a tree."

Sebastian straightened. "You gave something to a bird to hide?"

"Maybe?" Chloe tilted her head to the side. "Elena says it's time for me to go."

Sebastian's heart lurched. There was so much he wanted to tell her. "I'm sorry, Chloe. I wasn't there to protect you. I didn't get your message in time."

"Don't you dare." She punched his shoulder, hard. "Don't you dare blame this on yourself! You get all weepy over me, and I'll come haunt the shit out of you."

Sebastian brushed tears from his eyes. "You promise?"

Chloe rolled her eyes, then Elena blinked and looked at him. "I can't hear her. I think she doesn't have a lot of energy left."

The thought of his sister leaving, or never being able to talk to her again, hit him like a weight in the chest. He sat heavily on the couch, digesting what he'd seen. Then he looked at her. "Thank you. For giving me another chance to say goodbye."

Elena shrugged. "I am glad I could help. For once this gift is useful, rather than a nuisance."

That's when it clicked for him how drained she seemed. Her skin was pale, the bags under her eyes prominent. She hadn't yet moved from the couch, and he wondered if she even had the energy.

What does the possession do to her?

He was impressed all over again at her strength. How had she managed for so long?

Something clicked in his brain, and he hissed in a breath. "The research Chloe was talking about, it's at the Cain house, isn't it?"

Elena nodded. "One of the nests near the porch." The shadows grew longer on her face. "But before we go, there's one more thing I haven't told you yet." She explained about the creature that had been following her, how she'd been seeing it around town.

"I think I saw it too," he said, remembering the woman at the hospital.

"Bast, this shade, it's not like the others." She worried her hands together. "I'm not completely sure, but I think it's the same one that possessed my mother."

Edward.

He'd always wondered what had pushed Mrs. Cain over the edge. She'd never shown any real predilection for violence before that night.

And now I have a chance to catch the creature that was responsible.

A newfound sense of determination filled him. This was the chance he needed to make up for failing his siblings.

"I'm sorry I didn't tell you all of this sooner," Elena

said. "I share my mother's gift. I'm equally as susceptible as she is to the shades."

It was easy to read between the lines.

"You don't want what happened to Edward to happen to me," he said.

She kept all this pain to herself because she was protecting me.

He imagined her as the last warrior standing amid an army, covered in wounds, her armor dented, but refusing to yield.

My beautiful, brave warrior.

He sat beside her on the couch and pulled her into his arms.

"You don't have to do this alone," he said.

She shuddered, and then she was sobbing into his chest.

"That's right," he murmured. "Let me be strong for both of us."

Her sobs continued for what seemed like hours but was only a few minutes. He didn't care. For the first time since he'd seen Chloe's dead body, he felt like he was on even footing. Whatever else happened, Elena needed him.

And he would do whatever it took to make sure it stayed that way.

Chapter 14

Elena stretched, leaning against the rough bark of the tree, clutching the brush end of a broom in her hands. They'd already checked five nests, and her arm was sore from lifting it over her head.

So close. Just a little more.

"I've got a good feeling about this one," Sebastian said from the bottom of the ladder.

"Shush! I've almost got it. Get ready."

She tapped the bundle of sticks again. It shifted, then fell. She lowered her aching arm and craned her neck over the side of the ladder. The nest disintegrated as it fell, but all the pieces caught in the sheet they had strung up like a hammock between the neighboring trees.

As she clambered down the ladder, Sebastian started sifting through the debris.

"Well?" she asked. "Did we get it?"

He grinned and held out his palm. Sitting on it was a black square of plastic.

Finally, we can figure this out.

She picked up the micro-SD card with one hand and touched the back of her head with another.

"Come on," Sebastian said, tugging her arm. "I want to know what's on that thing."

She forced a smile, trying not to let him see how much her heart ached.

"Yeah. Let's go."

As they drove, the dread in her heart grew. Once they solved the case, there would be nothing stopping her from leaving. For a fleeting moment, she considered opening her window and chucking the tiny piece of plastic. But that wouldn't change anything. There was still a killer out there. She would only be delaying the inevitable.

So, she let Sebastian take the lead, holding his hand tightly in the elevator back up to his condo and then nodding and smiling as he dug through a pile of electronics for an adapter that would let him connect the card to his computer.

Then it was time, and when they finally saw what was on the card, she groaned. "That's it? Just one file?"

"Come on, Chloe," Sebastian whispered before double-clicking on *Research.docx.*

The screen loaded, revealing the file contained a single column of a dozen names.

And that was it.

"I don't understand," Sebastian said. "How does this help us?"

Everything they'd been through, all for a list of names.

Elena pulled her shirt away from her chest and looked down at the slitted snout of Chloe's boa.

Why did you hide this for us? Who are these people?

The boa did not respond.

"It must mean something," Sebastian said in a pained voice. "Let's look them up. Internet searches. Maybe it's a short list of suspects." Desperation lined his face. "That's better, right? Only a dozen people to investigate?"

She gulped. "Yeah, let's do it."

They made themselves comfortable in the living room and started researching. It didn't take long to find the connection between the names on the list.

"Listen to this," Elena said. "A highway patrol found Jordan Cooper, a student at the University of Minnesota, dead this morning alongside Highway 10. She was twenty-six years old and had been missing for two weeks. Jordan was traveling with a friend, Cara Rodriguez, who is still missing. Cara's brother, Julian, is also missing. Sources say Jordan's death is being treated as unexplained, and the investigation is ongoing."

She scrolled down the page to a photo of a young woman with dark hair and striking green eyes.

She looks just like Chloe.

"One of his victims," Sebastian said. "It has to be. Listen to this. I've got another one. Family members discovered Tanya Castle dead this morning just outside St. Cloud near Highway 10. Tanya, a sixteen-year-old, had left home two weeks prior and may have been hitchhiking across Minnesota. A representative from the St. Cloud police department reports that the investigation is ongoing."

Over the next hour, they learned that across the country, thousands of people disappeared every day. The missing often turned up the same day or week, misunderstandings between friends, teenage runaways, kids who wandered too far from their parents. A minority remained missing. Their cases stayed open for decades, their faces printed on billboards and milk cartons, pictures aged to represent the passage of time. Others were less lucky, kidnapped by friends or relatives, unaware anyone had been looking for them.

"Highway 10. That's the connection." Sebastian

shuddered. "That's where the killer is operating. He's picking up hitchhikers. He must be a trucker or someone who is on the road a lot."

Elena leaned back. "There's nothing here to tell us who the killer is." Relief warred with anger in her chest, and she sided with anger. "We're no closer to an answer than we were before. Dammit, Chloe!"

"Hey, it's okay," Sebastian said. He slid across the couch. "We'll figure this out. I told you, I won't let anything happen to you."

He wrapped his arms around her, and she melted into his embrace. He smelled earthy, like a campfire. Except the smoky scent was stronger than anything else, and as she breathed again, it tangled in her lungs and made her cough.

"What is that?" she asked, between coughing fits.

His arms tightened around her. "I think the building is on fire."

****

Smoke filled the room with impossible speed until Elena couldn't see a hand in front of her face.

They stumbled through the apartment, her hand clutching a belt loop on Sebastian's jeans. When they arrived at the front door, he rattled the door handle, then swore.

"It's jammed," he said. "Get back. I'll try to open it."

She shuffled away and heard the loud bang of Sebastian ramming his shoulder against the door twice before a coughing spasm sent him to his knees.

"It's no use," he said, finally. "Get down before you breathe in more smoke."

Remembering her fire lessons from childhood, she

got as low as she could, sliding her stomach on the floor and crawling forward along the carpet, coughing and squinting against the fumes. She kept one hand on Sebastian's boot, but with every minute, it was harder to see. She paused for a moment to rub her eyes, and he was gone.

"Sebastian!"

Her words were swallowed up by the crackling fire.

She grasped around, hoping she'd feel his hand on her arm or hear his voice. An image of him laying face down tormented her mind and brought tears to her eyes.

I can't lose him.

She wouldn't leave, not without making sure he was safe.

A vague shadow appeared in front of her, and she made for it, hoping it was him. Her fingers closed on an empty sleeve. It wasn't Sebastian, but his jacket. Her heart pounded with the effort of pulling air into her lungs. A crash to the right shocked her back into movement, and she scrambled away from the noise.

"Sebastian!" she screamed. The hot air scorched her throat.

"Elena?" His voice was a million miles away. "Where are you?"

The temperature continued to rise, but her skin wasn't hot. It was cold and clammy, like she was feverish. Her hand smacked something hard, the smooth edge of a door frame. She took a moment to rest, pulling in great gasps of air. She'd barely moved, and yet her muscles trembled as if she'd run a marathon.

Low oxygen.

The bathroom had a window to a fire escape, safety, freedom. She swayed to her feet. Once she judged it safe, she touched the door, finding it warm but not hot. She wrapped her hand in her shirt and pulled it open, holding her face away as a rush of air entered the hallway. A roar of sound followed, and a blast of heat seared her back, making her cry out.

"Elena!"

Sebastian's voice sent her heart soaring.

Hands grasped her shoulders.

"Sebastian?"

The hands shoved her, sending her flailing through the doorway. She turned, and the door slammed inches from her nose.

Under her feet was not the slick surface of tile but more carpet. She reached forward, and her fingers bumped against a solid wall.

"No, no, please, no!" Her arms splayed in all directions as she searched for some evidence to deny her growing suspicion.

Walls to the left and right within arm's length. She was not in the bathroom but in the hallway closet.

"No!"

She tried for the knob, but the door wouldn't budge. It was like something heavy was leaning against it from the other side, the same way the front door had been stuck. She took a step back and rammed her shoulder against the wood again and again until she was one large bruise. She slid down the door and wrapped her arms around her knees.

This is it. This is how I die.

She wailed. It was all her singed throat could manage. Her back ached, and she could barely move the fingers of her right hand.

A rich, coppery smell cut through the smoke, pulling

her into a memory.

Her mother plunged the knife into Edward's chest, again and again, splattering blood over the walls. Edward's head lolled to the side, and his eyes stared at her, unfocused.

"Mom, stop!" she sobbed. She rushed over to her mother's side and tried to pull her away, but her arm kept moving, up and down with that awful sucking sound.

She lowered her hands to the carpet. A sticky substance adhered to her fingers. She clambered away. Blood oozed from beneath the door and formed a puddle.

She turned and assaulted the wall, kicking and clawing, anything to escape the room and the ever-growing puddle of blood. She stared, horrified, at the lines of scarlet her bloody fingers had made on the wall.

She calmed her racing heart and took another look around. The blood had vanished.

It's not real.

Her searching fingers found a rod a foot above her head. Perfect. She shoved the few coats hanging from the rod to the floor, then yanked at it. Unfortunately for her, it had been screwed into the wall on both sides. She wiggled the metal back and forth until, finally, the screws creaked and turned. This triggered another frenzy until the rod finally broke away from the wall. The cool metal was firm and real in her grasp. She turned around. A light flickered from the crack between the door and wall. She placed one end of the rod in the gap and pulled, using the doorframe as a pivot point. The door moved. She pulled until her arms twitched and her lungs burned, until at last, there was enough room to squeeze through.

She stumbled forward blindly, screaming Sebastian's name between fits of coughing. Then hands grasped at her arms. She flailed, batting at her assailant.

"Stop, it's me."

It was too smoky to make out his expression, but his arms curled around her back. She shoved her head into his shoulder and sobbed. "Oh, God! I thought I'd lost you!"

"We have to get out of here," he said. "It's not just the fire. Someone tried to strangle me. I got free but lost them in the smoke."

She clung to his hand as he led them through a doorway. The change in texture beneath her feet confirmed they'd made it to the bathroom. Sebastian slammed the door behind them, and Elena soaked a towel in water from the running tap and then shoved it against the space where the door met the floor. Then she hit the switch to turn on the fan, although there wasn't much smoke in the bathroom.

That'll give us a few minutes.

Then they ran to the window and, after some grunting and effort, shoved it open. The rush of cool air on her face made her sob with relief. Fur brushed her fingers, and the cats squeezed past them, their frantic meowing cutting through the crackle of the fire. They descended the steps in a flash of orange and black, their nails making a tinkling sound against the metal grating.

"You got the cats," she rasped, her voice still rough.

"They're family," he replied.

Then the world exploded.

Chapter 15

The impact threw Elena against the wall. A sharp pain jabbed her leg, and her ears rang. She moved her body one muscle at a time.

Seconds later, the muted cry of sirens filled the air. She struggled to her feet. Sebastian stepped closer, and she grabbed his arm.

"Out!" she yelled over the noise of the fire. Her arms trembled, and she pushed through the exhaustion. Together they scrambled onto the fire escape.

Arms enveloped her, and she panicked for a moment before realizing it was a firefighter. They pressed a plastic mask against her face, and clean air filled her lungs.

"Thank you," she rasped.

Sebastian guided her to an ambulance, where a paramedic draped a blanket over her shoulder. For shock, they said. Across the street from the ambulance, the tall building they'd escaped from blazed. The flames licked the roof of the apartment building next door. The fire had singed her hair, and streaks of soot covered her body. She'd been lucky. Her lungs ached from the ash and smoke she had breathed in, but she would live.

The next few minutes passed in a haze. A plaintive meowing from the corner of the ambulance told her a kind soul had gathered the cats. She glanced over to see a crude box with a few holes poked into it.

She made to rise, but her legs were rubbery like a newborn calf.

Then Sebastian was in front of her. His face was stained with soot, and there were bags under his eyes. She'd never seen anything more beautiful in her life. His lips moved, but a high-pitched note drowned out his voice.

She seized his arm and squeezed, willing blood back to her hands. She was so cold. He pulled her close, wrapping the edge of the blanket around them both. Shielded from the outside, she pressed her face into his shoulder and tried not to think about what they'd lost. Sebastian's home, his clothing, countless mementos. Her anger burned with the same intensity as the inferno. He squeezed her tight, and she closed her eyes, letting the warmth of his chest sink into her chilled skin.

We're both alive and together. That's all that matters.

"What now?" she whispered. Her eyes were dry of tears. The fire had taken them, too. Was it time to give up? Retreat and fight another day?

"Now we find the son of a bitch who did this," he said. Then he pressed his lips to her forehead in a gentle caress. There was no use pretending the fire was an accident. There was no way Sebastian had trapped her inside the closet.

Although she had a sneaking suspicion the report would list the cause as unexplained or electrical.

The wind shifted and drifted ash and smoke over them, making her cough. Sebastian pulled her into the relative safety of the ambulance. He tilted her head toward him with one blanket-enclosed hand and searched her eyes. They met in the middle with a kiss that sent electricity sparking through Elena's veins. She relaxed into his embrace and enjoyed a lazy duel, surrendering to his dominance. His large hand moved around her shoulder, down her back, around her hip. He squeezed, and a liquid heat pooled and spilled over. A fit of coughing interrupted the moment, and Elena hacked up a black substance onto the metal floor.

"You need a doctor. I'll be back." Sebastian ran out into the crowd.

She shivered in delayed fear. Great plumes of smoke rose into the sky like black clouds, staining it an inky black.

"They won't give up," she whispered to herself. "They'll keep coming after me until I am dead."

"Unless you do something about it."

She jumped at the voice. A man stood in the shadows. Most of his body was hidden beneath a large trench coat, the hood pulled up over his head.

"Who—"

With a pop and a rush of air, a shade manifested on her stomach. She peeked beneath her clothing. It was a wolf spider, the same shade she'd seen on her attacker at Chloe's house.

"It's you!" she cried. "You attacked me!"

She pushed herself deeper into the ambulance, ready to scream or barricade herself inside.

"Relax. I'm not here to fight," the man said.

A pins and needles sensation began on her back, but she ignored it. The spider wouldn't get the best of her, not when she was so angry.

"Well, what the hell do you want, then? To kill me, like you killed Chloe?"

She glanced over his shoulder, but Sebastian was

nowhere in sight, and the police and firefighters were too far away. She searched the metal floor of the ambulance behind her with her fingertips. If she could find something to strike him with, distract him, then maybe there was a radio inside she could use to call for help.

The man laughed. "Me? A killer? No. I was trying to get you to leave, to get you out of my way, but apparently, that hasn't worked."

Get me out of the way?

"The goggles and the phone call? That was you?"

The man nodded. "You didn't take the hint. Now the man who killed Chloe is after you, too."

Elena's heart thumped in her chest. "You know who killed Chloe?"

"Unfortunately, no. I thought she might've hidden her research in her house, but it wasn't there. Then you showed up." For the first time, the man's voice sounded angry. "I couldn't have you blabbing to the cops. Not when I am so close."

She remembered the description of the man Chloe met at the bowling alley. "You were her contact. Is that what you were doing, trying to catch the murderer?"

Thumping footsteps drew closer. The man tensed. "You really need to come with me." He checked his watch. "Last chance."

Elena closed her fingers around something long and smooth, with a sharp tip. A discarded needle. It wasn't ideal, but it was a better weapon than her own nails.

Then a ball of fire erupted from the building, and the man flinched. Elena lunged forward, but before she could get within a foot of the man, a fierce pounding began in her head, and she was ripped out of her body. The restraints coiled around her, pulling her until she could see only a dim view of the world outside.

"Suit yourself," the man said. "I'll come for you when it's over." Then he stepped back into the shadows.

The ambulance door swung in the wind, and she caught a glance of her face in the glass, the jagged teeth in her mouth.

The Harvester had found her.

Then her body turned, and she realized Sebastian was running toward her.

No! Sebastian, run away! Don't come near me!

Even without a physical body, she soon tired of thrashing. She watched, helplessly, as Sebastian wrapped her in a hug.

The shade lowered her hand holding the needle, tucking it behind her back.

"You shouldn't be walking around," he said. "The paramedic said you inhaled a lot of smoke."

The creature inside her body didn't respond.

Run. Please run. Her heart ached at the thought of what was coming.

"There's something I have to show you," the shade said. "Come on."

As Elena watched, screaming at the shade to leave, it led Sebastian into the back of the ambulance and then closed the doors.

"What is it? Are you hurt somewhere else?" The concern on Sebastian's face ripped at Elena's heart.

"It's the cats," the shade said, pointing to the box in the corner. "I think Tiger was hurt."

"If it'll make you feel better, I'll take a quick look," Sebastian said. Then he fell to his knees in front of the box.

The shade raised the hand holding the needle.

No!

****

Sebastian spun around just in time to dodge the strike. Elena stumbled past him and slammed heavily into a cabinet. Bandages and bottles fell from the shelves and shattered onto the ground, spraying liquid that had a strong astringent smell, like cleanser.

"Elena, what—"

She pivoted toward him and lunged again; an uncapped needle clenched tightly in her fist. The whites of her eyes were stained with black, and she panted like a dog. She bared her teeth, and for a second, they were jagged and sharp.

She's possessed by a shade.

Except instead of Chloe, this was a much more terrible creature.

He grabbed for her hand holding the needle, but she twisted out of his grip.

"Almost, but not quite," she said. Then she uttered a cackling laugh that made the hairs on the back of his neck rise. "If I'd known this would be so fun, I would've done it ages ago."

"I know you're in there, Elena," Sebastian said, meeting her eyes. "Fight, damn it! Don't let this thing control you."

"Oh, that's good," the creature crooned. "What next? How 'bout a nice long cuddle? We can all sit down and talk about our feelings." It cackled again as if entertained by its own taunt, and then bounced from foot to foot like a maniacal jester, tossing the needle from one hand to the next.

Sebastian darted forward, but the creature danced away, hopping onto a stretcher, then back to the floor.

"Not a chance, not a chance," it said in a sing-song voice. "Now that I've got control, she's all mine. Won't be letting go, no thank you. Never going back again." Then it slashed with the needle, nearly skewering him.

Time for Plan B.

He snagged the heavy blanket, the one the paramedics had wrapped around Elena's shoulders, with his toe. When the creature moved next, he jerked forward and enveloped Elena's upper body in the fabric, then slapped his hand over her mouth and nose. The creature struggled, bucking and screaming, but Sebastian held tight. No matter the paranormal nature of the possession, it was occupying a human body, which meant finite strength. Maybe if it had taken over a bodybuilder or another cop, then he'd be in trouble, but Elena was no match for him.

The creature's struggling slowed and then stilled.

Thank God.

He carefully lowered Elena's body to the floor, being sure she didn't hit her head. He didn't have long, maybe a minute, before she revived. There had to be something in the ambulance he could use to knock her out or restrain her until Elena regained control. He shoved open drawers and threw supplies onto the floor until he finally found a pair of zip ties.

He spun around and removed the blanket. The creature grinned with its awful, sharpened teeth.

"Missed you," it said, with a wink and a kissing face.

Before he could react, the creature smashed a heavy object against his temple. He crumpled to the ground and clutched his head. When he lifted his fingers, they were coated in blood.

"This was fun, but I'm more of a ladies' man," the

creature said. "So, it's time to end this."

A blanket fell over him, the same one he'd used to restrain the creature. He raised his hands, but it was too late. The creature clamped its hands over his nose and mouth until his vision went black.

The next thing he knew, he was sprawled on the floor of the ambulance, his head aching, cocooned in a blanket. He threw it off and pushed to a sitting position.

Elena stood near the door, her face pale. "What have I done?" she whispered as if she didn't realize she was speaking. Tears streamed down her cheeks.

Sebastian struggled to his feet. "It wasn't you. It was that thing."

Elena wiped away her tears. "It doesn't matter. I almost killed you! If it weren't for me—" she broke off, shaking her head. "Now you know why I can't stay with you."

He reached for her hand. "Elena that's not—"

But she was already gone.

Chapter 16

Elena fled the ambulance, leaving Sebastian before a shade could possess her again and finish the job. She still couldn't believe what the Harvester had almost made her do. Had she been a moment slower in regaining control, Sebastian would've followed his brother, sister, and Elena's mother into death.

You were right, Aunt Martha. It's not safe for me to be out in society.

The worst part was that she'd had plenty of opportunities to prevent what had happened. She hadn't imagined it. The Harvester really had been following her since she left the city. Toying with her.

She walked along the empty streets, furiously wiping the tears from her cheeks and thinking back to all the times she'd thought the Harvester was nearby and had dismissed it. She'd been so obsessed with finding Chloe's killer that she'd ignored her instincts.

Never again.

She passed an alley. The man in the trench coat was there. Her aunt's emissary. He grinned.

"Are you ready to go home now?"

Elena trudged toward him with her head bowed. "Yes."

A black limo pulled up next to them, and the man walked past her to open the back door. Elena climbed inside and, when the man didn't join her, stretched out along the long seat, burying her face in her hands.

Admitting defeat stung, but it was better than risking the lives of the people she loved.

I'll keep telling myself that until I believe it.

When the car finally stopped, the car door opened again, and she stepped into an underground parking garage. It was large as an airplane hangar, with concrete columns set every ten feet, but there were only a few other cars dispersed throughout the space.

The man exited the car from the passenger seat and gestured for her to follow him. They walked through the empty concrete jungle into an open doorway and then down a narrow hall that exited into a small room. The walls were flat white, and the floors were polished marble tile. The bright halogens in the ceiling left ghostly circles in her vision, and she had to blink a few times before her eyes adjusted.

There was a four-poster queen bed in the corner, the mattress bare except for three piles of neatly folded sheets, towels, and soft-looking blankets. A side table next to the bed held a silver lamp with a plain white shade, and an open door opposite the one she'd entered led to what looked like a bathroom with a sink and a toilet. But despite the relative luxury of her surroundings, a heavy weight settled on her shoulders.

So, this is my new prison.

"You can wait here," the man said before exiting and closing the door behind him. She didn't bother to check it. What was the point? There was nowhere for her to go. She walked over to the bed and sat down.

There was a knock at the door, and a young Hispanic woman entered the small room.

"*Buenos días,*" the woman said. "Good morning.

My name is Dr. Rodriguez. I'll be overseeing your care during your stay at Haven."

That name rang a bell. Hadn't she heard it before? "Rodriguez. Cara Rodriguez?"

The doctor took a half step back. "*Sí*. Yes, that is me. How did you know?"

"You're one of the missing women Chloe was researching."

Cara's face paled.

"What? What's wrong?" Elena asked.

Cara's eyes darted around the room, and then she shook her head. "You must not speak that name here."

Yet more secrets.

"Why? How do you know Chloe?"

Cara made a shushing motion. "I'm sorry. I must not say more."

Elena wanted to push her, demand what Cara knew, but she shoved those impulses away. It would do no good. The incident with Sebastian had proved she could not live out in the world. The best thing she could do was quickly adapt to her new surroundings.

Her prison.

Cara placed a hand on her arm and made a noise like a thousand crickets chirping at once. Her mouth dropped open, and a white foam dropped from her lips. Her eyes rolled back, and she spoke in a baritone voice that chilled Elena to the bone.

"He is close. Watching, waiting for his chance. He will stop at nothing to consume you."

Then the doctor released her grip and staggered backward, clutching her head. "What just happened?"

Elena shifted on the bed. "You touched me, then something strange happened."

Cara winced. "I see. *Lo siento.* What happened before I touched you?"

"You were introducing yourself," Elena said. "You really can't remember?"

Cara crossed her arms. "It is the curse of my gift. When I touch people, I see things about them. Sometimes past, sometimes future. *Según.* It depends. But each time it happens, I lose some of my own memories." She straightened. "This does not matter. Please, come with me. The others wish to speak with you."

Still reeling from the realization that there were others like her, Elena resisted the urge to ask a thousand questions and followed her prison guard back through the dark hallway. They stopped at a closed door, and Cara unlocked it with a key she removed from her pocket. The door opened to reveal another hallway. Elena stepped through. The doctor gave her an encouraging smile, then closed the door.

I guess I do this on my own.

She walked forward and made out the voices of two women arguing.

"You can't keep her here. She's a target."

"She is one of us."

Elena's steps faltered.

Were they talking about her? What would she do if they kicked her out? She had nowhere else to go.

"What do we do then?" the first voice continued. "Let her go free and expose our position? After everything we've done?"

Unwilling to eavesdrop any longer, Elena stepped into the light. A half a dozen middle-aged women sat in wingback chairs in a circular living room. There were no windows, but the ceiling was several stories high.

The group turned to face her as one.

A woman sitting at the fringes of the group had a black crow perched on her shoulder. A jolt of surprise rocked Elena. "Aunt Martha. Jelly?"

The crow squawked and fluttered off her aunt's shoulder. It shimmered and grew, contorting until it took the shape of an orange tomcat.

"Tiger?"

The cat meowed and shimmered again, growing into the shape of a woman with silvery hair that flowed around her shoulders in loose ringlets. A young boy hurried up to the woman and handed her a pile of dove gray fabric.

"Curses," she said as she donned the gown. "I always forget how large my breasts are in this form." She smiled at Elena. "I am sorry for the deception. My name is Ethel. I'm a friend of your aunt."

Another fact slotted into place in her mind. "That's why you let me leave. You were following me the whole time."

First as a crow, then as a cat.

Martha stood, a look of sadness on her face. "I am so sorry, dear. It was the only way. We had to make sure you wouldn't turn."

Elena looked back and forth between the women, not understanding. "What are you talking about?"

Ethel cleared her throat. "There is, I mean, there was, a device in your body, placed a long time ago. We had to ensure it was removed. We could not have you tracked here."

Elena glared at her aunt. "That was you. I know it was. Why did you do that to me?"

Martha flushed. "We knew what your mother had done. It seemed the only way."

Ethel sighed. "We had to watch you. It was not safe for you to be out on your own, not when we did not know what you were capable of. It was never our intention to harm you. But you must understand why we did it. We had to make sure you would not succumb, as your mother did."

"Did you kill Chloe?" Elena asked, her voice breaking.

Ethel shook her head. "No. We don't know who did that, I'm afraid."

"Oh." Elena slumped. "So, what happens now?"

"Now, you stay with us."

The other women murmured their dissent, and Martha's smile cracked for the first time.

"I'm sorry, Martha," Ethel said. "But you've been outvoted. The girl cannot stay with us. With that creature focused on her, it's too dangerous. We have lost so many already."

Elena looked up from where she'd been staring at her feet. "So many?"

Martha closed her eyes, her expression pained. "So many of our brothers and sisters. As soon as we find them, we dispatch a messenger, but sometimes it is too late."

Ethel walked over and put an arm around Martha, then looked at Elena. "Your friend, Chloe, stumbled upon our secret. Someone is targeting the gifted we are trying to protect."

Elena's anger sizzled and crackled at the implications of those words. "You knew Chloe was in danger, but you did nothing to protect her. You sat here, hiding from the world while those women died." She looked around the room, but none of the women would look her in the eye. Martha returned to her seat.

Elena scowled at the collective women. Sitting in their chairs, not even trying to fight, they'd buried themselves in the ground. Once, she would have sided with them. Not anymore.

"I'm done here."

She returned the way she'd come.

Cara was waiting in the room, clutching her hands together. "You can't go back."

"I can do anything I want."

The doctor rubbed her fists together. "You're putting him in danger."

Elena hesitated mid-retort. Cara was right. Sebastian would always be at risk if he stayed with her. She sat on the bed, head in her hands.

"How can I go on?" she whispered. "I love him." The truth settled over her and made her ache.

"We've all had to leave those we love," Cara said.

"You lost someone?"

Cara took a shuddering breath. "My brother. He disagreed with the life we made here."

"And you don't?"

"*Esta es mi casa.*" She shrugged. "This is the only home I know. The world outside holds only pain for me."

A tap on her shoulder. Elena turned toward a burly man carrying a small black bag. He held it out to her, and she took it. "What do I do with this?"

He mimed putting the bag over his head, and she groaned.

Not again.

****

"What is the nature of your relationship with Elena Cain?"

Roth's voice was tense with repressed excitement.

"We're friends."

The detective tapped the table with his fingers. "What about Jordan Cooper? Cara Rodriguez? Tanya Castle? Were you friends with them, too?"

The missing people Chloe was investigating.

"I'm the victim here," Sebastian said. He hit the table with his palm. "My building burned down. I was almost killed!"

Roth shifted in his seat. "That's for another division to investigate. I'm a homicide cop. Now, tell me about your relationship with Ms. Cain."

Sebastian groaned. The detective was hell-bent on peppering him with banal questions. They'd gone around in circles for hours, and it was only desperation to learn what had happened to Elena that kept him from ending the interview. He had to get back to Elena, convince her she hadn't hurt him, that the possession wasn't her fault. He tapped his foot on the ground.

Roth flipped a few pages in his notebook. "Where were you at three am?"

"Why?"

"We need to establish if you have an alibi."

"I was at home," Sebastian said. "Asleep."

Triumph flashed in Roth's eyes. He leaned forward. "And last Tuesday, mid-afternoon. Where were you then?"

Sebastian scowled. "I was driving. On the way to the Cain house. You know this already. It's in my statement. Not to mention you showed up shortly after. Roth, tell me what's going on. Have you found new evidence?"

The detective hesitated, then removed a photo from the back of his notebook and placed it on the table. A woman lay face down on the grass, her hair fanned around her face like a mane. Chloe.

"Why are you showing me this?" his voice was rough with emotion. "I was there. I found her."

Roth placed another picture on the table. A pale, lifeless face with cloudy eyes. From the state of her body, she had been dead for some time.

"What is this?" he whispered, grabbing the picture with numb fingers.

"We found her this morning. Is she another of your victims?"

"What?" Sebastian dropped the picture. "You think I did this?"

Roth's voice grew in volume as he continued, "How did you do it? Ask them to meet you, then drown them? Did they struggle? Did they beg for their lives before you killed them? Where are the others, Castillo? What have you done with them?"

How could he reason with the man?

"I didn't kill her. I didn't kill any of them. Why would I?"

The situation was getting out of control. Roth leaned forward, grinning like a satisfied cat. "You told me yourself. Chloe was investigating these cases. I think she figured out what you were doing, and you killed her before she could tell anyone."

"That's ridiculous."

Before Roth could respond, someone slammed on the glass, and he changed course. "Did you kill Elena, too? Is that why she's gone missing?"

Missing.

Finally, Roth had slipped up. Unfortunately, the news did little to calm Sebastian's nerves. "That's enough," he said. "I won't answer any more questions. I want a lawyer."

Roth laughed but rose from his chair, shoving it back with a metallic screech that made Sebastian cringe. "Lawyer, huh? You'll need one." He walked out and slammed the door.

Sebastian was still staring at the table when the door opened and a man in a tailored black suit and slicked-back hair entered. With a casual motion, he unplugged the camera in the corner and a second camera near the door.

"I am only doing this as a favor to Elena," the man said, taking the seat recently vacated by Roth and flipping the pictures on the table over. "We don't need them watching us."

Sebastian resisted the urge to grab the pictures, to keep them away from the well-dressed stranger. "Do I know you?"

The man placed a briefcase on the table. "No. I'll be your legal representation. David Smythe."

So this is Elena's attorney.

David leaned forward. "Did you kill those women?"

Straight to the point. A refreshing change. Sebastian's shoulders slumped. "No."

David nodded. "I believe you. Do you know where Elena is?"

"No. Do you?"

David shook his head, then his features tightened. "But I'll find her. She can't hide forever."

What does that mean?

The door clicked open, and Roth walked in, his face

marred by a frown.

"Let me handle this," David said. He straightened to his full height and towered over the detective. "Are you filing charges against my client?"

Roth gave them an icy stare but said nothing as they left the interrogation room. When they were outside the station, and Sebastian had his phone back, he turned it on and checked his messages.

Nothing.

Chapter 17

The car dropped Elena off a mile from town, ostensibly so no one could follow it back to Haven.

She followed the instructions the surly guard gave her and counted to a hundred before removing the bag from her head. Then she crumpled the black velvet material in her hands. What would have happened if another car had driven by? Would they have stopped and come to her aid? Or did the locals know to leave people by the side of the road to themselves? She imagined a station wagon going down the highway. The woman would glance out and see her as they passed, then cluck her tongue and say, "Another one. What is this town coming to?"

Elena shook her head and began her walk into town. She still had her phone and her wallet if things went wrong.

Her phone. Sebastian. She pulled out her phone and turned it on. As it powered up, she peered down the highway. A sign in the distance glinted in the sunlight.

Highway 10.

The road where the police found the missing women. Wasn't that interesting? Her hand buzzed. She had four voicemails. She let them play, having a good idea of what she would hear.

"Elena, it's Sebastian. Call when you get this."

"Hey, it's me again. Call me."

"Elena, what's going on? Call me, please. I'll be waiting."

"Where are you? Call me, and I'll come pick you up."

Heart aching, she started to dial Sebastian's number when her fingers hesitated. Cara's words echoed in her mind. He would never be safe with her. She put her phone back into her pocket.

There was only one place she could go.

****

Somehow, it wasn't a surprise to find Chloe's car tucked into the corner of the parking lot, where no one would notice it.

Too tired to deal with the car, she sent a quick email to Sandra asking her to report the car to the station. From what Elena could see, the vehicle was wiped clean. Again, her enemy had been careful.

She looked up and took in the wide grassy field dotted with gray shapes like polka dots on the horizon. She walked along the beaten gravel path with no need to know where to go.

The path diverged, again and again, worn patterns testament to those remembered. She continued to walk until she found her mother's resting place. A granite stone set in the ground listed her name. Simple, what her mother would have wanted.

"I miss you."

The cold, wet grass seeped through her jeans and chilled her legs. She touched the smooth stone.

"Mom, I need your guidance." She summoned an image of her mother and held it in her mind. Waist-length brown hair, hazel eyes, and a smile that dazzled anyone who met her. Unlike Elena, she had never stared, never recoiled when offered a hand. Her control had been absolute.

Until the Harvester had taken her.

The thought evoked a fresh wave of guilt. Tears dripped down her cheeks.

"I don't know what to do. I can't stay because he'll find me again and hurt Sebastian. But I can't just leave, not after what happened to Chloe. She deserves justice."

The wind rustled a nearby tree, startling a family of crows into flight. She watched them fly and depart until they became black smudges in the distance. The clouds above shifted, and a ray of sunlight illuminated the ground. A transparent form of a red fox flickered into view. Elena scrambled backward. Beady black eyes blinked, and she was thrust into a memory.

Three men in dark raincoats lowered the casket into the grave, putting an end to weeks of hope. The rain pattered a solemn staccato upon rows and rows of black umbrellas that hid the mournful faces of so many her mother had touched during her life.

Tears welled up, but she refused to let them go, choosing to view the world through a hazy sheen. After days of silence and an aching emptiness in her heart, the pain of her grief breached the defenses around her heart.

Without warning, the memory changed. A sound buzzed at the back of her mind, and her world expanded.

"It's time to let go." A woman's voice. Her mother's voice.

"Mom!"

She spun around, searching for her mother's silhouette among the grieving. The people standing in front of her shuffled around and looked at her, sympathy written on their expressions.

Elena backed away from the crowd, then whispered. "Mom?"

"Yes, dear, it's me."

Tears leaked out of Elena's eyes. "How is this possible?"

A gentle sigh. "I couldn't leave you."

"Where are we? Is this the past?"

"No, dear, just a memory. You are not yet strong enough for me to talk to you any other way."

Elena's arm itched. She slid back her sleeve and found a fox shade curled above her wrist.

"I'm so sorry, love. I never wanted to leave you. I tried, I swear, but he was too strong."

"Oh, mom," she kept her voice low, not wanting to disturb the mourners.

Then again, what did it matter? It wasn't real. Her body was probably still in the graveyard, collapsed on the ground, or staring off into space like she was on tranquilizers.

Still, it felt disrespectful. She hid behind a tree, pressing her back to the rough wood. The fox on her forearm licked its paw and rubbed the side of its face. The shade stopped moving and looked at her. A question flew from her lips before she could think.

"How did he beat you, mom? You were so strong. Was it my fault? Did you spend all your energy keeping me from getting in trouble?"

"You know that's not why."

"Then how?"

"I'm almost out of time. It pains me to do this to you, but there's something important you need to know."

"I'm ready."

"I'm so proud of you, love. You've become such a

beautiful, smart young woman. I wish I had been there to see you grow up."

Emotion clogged her throat. She rubbed her nose on her sleeve. "Why didn't you become a shade? Then we could have stayed together."

"It's not that simple."

"You can't leave me like this. Why show up at all if you are just going to leave right away?"

"Don't take that tone with me, young lady. I'm still your mother."

Elena laughed, tears tumbling down her cheeks "You haven't changed."

The world tilted sideways, and she was back in the present. The fox rubbed its nose with a paw and then bunched its hindquarters and jumped, vanishing into her chest. It happened so quickly, she didn't have a chance to scream. She peeked beneath her shirt to see the fox perched above Chloe's boa, its tail curled around its toes.

At least you stayed with me.

She wiped the tears from her cheeks, rose, and slapped the grass and dead leaves from her legs. She looked down at her mother's gravestone and a chill washed over her.

The date had previously read "1961 - 1999" had a scratch running through 1999, and above it was written 2015.

****

Elena had walked five miles and was just beginning to see the fringes of town when a white SUV pulled to the side of the road. A man in an immaculate suit stepped out.

"Elena! I worried something had happened to you." He enveloped her in a tight hug.

"Good to see you too, David." She patted his back.

He'd aged since she'd seen him last. His once black hair was shot through with silver at the temples. His suit masked some of the weight he'd gained, but she could see it, a smoothing out of hard edges. Only his eyes were the same; an intense, piercing blue.

She was not used to seeing people she knew age. It scared her.

A shade on his neck twitched its nose. An arctic hare. She sent it a mental warning to stay away. She'd had her fill of dealing with shades for a long time. She cleared her throat. David was stretching a friendly hug into something uncomfortable. He pulled away, skin flushed.

"Come on, we need to get you out of here." He gestured to the car.

They drove past town into Minneapolis. David insisted on paying for a hotel room when he learned Sebastian's building had gone up in flames.

"How did you know where to find me?" She tried to keep her voice casual.

David laughed. "I know you better than you think."

They parked in the parkade and made their way into one of the nicest hotels she had ever seen. While David dealt with reception, she wandered around the lobby. A fancy coffee machine sat in a corner next to a collection of porcelain mugs. She made herself a latte and sat in a plush divan to watch a TV mounted in the ceiling. A young reporter was covering the fire. In one wide-angle shot of the smoldering building, Sebastian stood at the fringes of the crowd. Her fingers clutched her mug, and she was reminded of the messages on her phone.

David appeared and handed her a key card. "Room

431."

They took the elevator up to the fourth floor, and once in the spacious room, she looked around and huffed. "I would have been fine with a motel."

David waved a hand. "Nonsense." His posture was stiff. An uncomfortable silence filled the room.

"You're not telling me something. What do you know?"

The hare from earlier swam into life on his neck. She frowned. Its silver fur was stained with black. She peered closer, but the shade faded out of view. David walked past her and opened the door.

Sebastian stood there.

"I'll leave you two to get reacquainted," David said. He dashed out of the room.

"Where were you?" Sebastian asked. "Why didn't you answer your phone? I was so worried."

His words were daggers in her heart. Instead of answering, she grabbed his lapels and kissed him, drinking in the heat of him. She wound her arms around his neck, and he drew her taut against him, one hand cradling her neck, the other pressed to the small of her back.

They stumbled into the bedroom.

She ran her nails down his back. His arms tightened around her until it was almost painful. Interesting. Curious how far she could take this play, she pressed her nails deeper. Not enough to draw blood, but enough to make temporary indentations in his flesh. A strangled moan was her reward.

"You like that?" she ran her tongue along the curve of his ear. In answer, he hiked her thigh up to his hip, pressing his hardness against her center. "What do you think?"

He forced her back against the wall, crushing his mouth to hers, willing her to surrender.

Elena wrapped a leg around his hip and pulled him closer. He nipped at her lips until she opened them, then laid claim to her mouth.

The onslaught of attention made her knees weak, and she slid down the wall. He grunted and released her hands, moving them to her hips, pulling her tight against his chest.

The heat of his body thrilled her senses. He pushed her against the wall once again, cushioning the impact with his arms. She growled and threaded her fingers through his hair, then led a trail of gentle nips along his neck, stopping where his pulse was strongest and sucking. Sebastian gasped and thrust against her, the hard jut of his arousal pressing against her center. She chuckled and grasped the edge of his shirt, pulling it up and over his chest. The tanned expanse of skin gave her so very many ideas. She nipped his shoulder, just hard enough for him to feel it.

"That's enough, you minx," Sebastian said, his voice low.

His weight pinned her. He shifted, and she unbuttoned his trousers, then jerked them down and curled her fingers around him.

"God!"

She moved her fingers carefully up and down.

He groaned and closed his eyes. Sweat beaded along his skin.

"Oh, he likes that," she said.

Warm hands traveled down her sides and squeezed. "You ready? Cause you're killing me. I'm ready to burst."

"What are you waiting for, then?"

****

Sebastian positioned himself against her entrance and pushed inside, loving the wet slickness of her lips clutching him. He hissed in pleasure and resisted the urge to thrust inside. She deserved better than that. A moment later, she wrapped her legs around his hips and did the deed for him, pulling him deep. She moaned a guttural sound that drove him to the brink.

He set a slow rhythm, one that frustrated them both. She moved beneath him, squeezing him closer with her legs, forcing him to increase his pace until they were both panting with the need for release. A quirk of her lips warned him something was coming. She squeezed her sheath around him, and the pressure made his vision darken at the edges. With one final thrust, he came inside of her.

When the ecstasy dimmed, he rolled over and trailed his hands down her side. "Want help?"

She smiled. "Put your fingers in me."

He slid one finger inside her, then another. She was still so tight and wet that his cock stirred even so soon after spending himself.

Her head fell back. "Thrust in and out. Oh, yes, just like that." She tensed, and he continued the motion until she quivered around his fingers.

"God, I want to feel that on my cock."

A blush rose on her cheeks. "Maybe next time." She curled up next to him, using his shoulder as a pillow.

Chapter 18

The bitter aroma of coffee drew Elena to the small kitchenette where Sebastian stood, wearing a pair of low-waisted jeans and nothing else.

She appreciated the view, imagining running her hands along the long planes of his back, the muscle shifting beneath her fingers. Water dripped down his shoulders from his damp hair. She longed to lick that water away.

A shade flickered into being.

"Oh, my."

The shade filled the entirety of Sebastian's back, a tawny lion, mouth open in a roar. She took a step closer, entranced by the vividness of its colors.

He turned and smiled at her. She forgot the lion; crystallized his expression into memory.

"Afternoon. Hope you don't mind. I thought I'd surprise you. This hotel room must have cost David a fortune. There was a fully stocked fridge!"

He lifted bacon from a pan on the stove to a plate. The smell made her mouth water. He caught her looking and smirked. "Hungry again?"

"Shut it, you."

He tilted a perfect tomato and cheddar omelet onto the plate.

"Is this what you're always like in the morning?" she asked.

He winked. "Only when I wake up next to a beautiful woman."

Uncertain how to respond, she cut a piece of omelet and stuck it in her mouth, resolving to compliment him regardless of how it tasted. An unfamiliar tangy flavor hit her tongue. "Ohm-god," she said, her mouth full. "So good!"

He beamed. "My grandmother's secret recipe." He pulled out a chair and joined her. Their legs were so close she could feel the heat of his thighs. She ran his foot along his shin.

"Coffee?" she rose from her chair.

Sebastian waved a hand for her to stay. "I got it." He poured them both cups, hers without milk or sugar.

He remembered. Her stomach fluttered with affection.

Sebastian took a sip from his mug. "I'm wondering what we do next."

"Must you?"

He stared at her.

She sighed. "Just once, I wish I didn't have to bother about all of this." She stole a piece of bacon from his plate and chomped on it. "Outside those walls, so many things are waiting for me. But in here," she took his hand and squeezed. "It's just us. Two people eating breakfast together. No killers or ghosts or shady organizations. I wish it could stay like this."

The pained look in Sebastian's eyes cut her to the core. She slipped her hand away, but he caught it with both of his.

"It can. Sandra could get us new passports. We could leave the country."

She shook her head. "I've tried that. It doesn't work.

You just keep running, forever. It gets really tiring."

"Okay," he said. "Then let's do this. Whatever it is, we'll figure it out. Together."

"Agreed," she said, her heart swelling at the thought.

A knock at the door interrupted the moment.

"Ignore it," she said, kissing his neck.

Another knock, and then a soft voice called. "Housekeeping."

Sebastian groaned. "I'll flip the do not disturb sign over." He kissed her once on the lips, then again on the cheek. "You need anything?"

She fell back onto the couch. "Some ice, if you don't mind." She touched the back of her head. "It still aches."

****

Sebastian picked up his discarded robe from the back of a chair in the kitchen and shrugged it on. Less for warmth and more to avoid housekeeping staff from spying on his raging erection.

God, Elena.

He'd never been so consistently aroused, not since he was a teen. Every touch, every look she gave him made his pulse race. Even after spending himself several times over the past few hours, the thought of her languishing in his arms made him hard as a rock.

He closed the robe around his waist and grabbed the ice bucket from on top of the kitchenette counter. The door to their suite was propped open by the latch, so he assumed whoever had knocked on their door had bustled inside, although he didn't see any carts.

Probably giving us more towels or something.

He made sure his hotel key was in his robe pocket, then exited out into the hallway, not bothering to put on shoes or the flimsy slippers the hotel had provided with the robes. With the ice bucket tucked under his arm, he followed the soft humming sound until he found the huge black machine at the end of the hall. He placed the bucket beneath the dispenser and was about to press the lever when a voice spoke.

"How is she?"

He turned to see David standing in the middle of the hallway, his hands clasped behind his back, a look of concern written across his face.

"She's been through a lot," Sebastian replied. "We both have."

David grimaced. "I should've come back sooner. I owed her that much."

Sebastian hit the lever, waited until it was full of ice, then faced Elena's lawyer. "Why? You're not her father."

A pained look crossed David's face before he sighed. "I promised her mother I would look out for her, but keeping an eye on her is a full-time job."

Sebastian shuffled the ice bucket. David's admission reminded him of Chloe, how he'd tried so hard to watch over her after Edward's death.

"For what it's worth, I don't think she blames you for anything that happened," Sebastian said. He remembered what Chloe had told him through Elena's body. "And it's not too late. There's still a killer."

David frowned. "You're not going after him on your own, are you? I can't support such a foolish action."

"Suit yourself," Sebastian said, passing David. He reached for his key card to unlock the door, juggling the ice bucket. He got the door open and took two steps inside when a searing pain started in his chest. It was so intense like he'd been doused in gasoline and set on fire.

The ice bucket thumped to the floor. He screamed, but no sound came out. His body continued to move, but he couldn't control it.

He fought back a rising tide of panic that threatened to drown him until suddenly he wasn't in the hotel but surrounded by a dense mist.

Pretty awful when all you can do is watch, isn't it? A soft voice in his head whispered. *I'm so tired of watching. Trust me, this is better.*

He tried to talk and remembered he couldn't.

Don't bother, the voice continued. *It took me ages to figure out how to break myself from that monster. You're not going anywhere until he's done with you.*

The mist thinned, and a small rabbit hopped out. Its body was white but with large splotches of gray on its hips and ears. It rose on its hind legs and sniffed the air. *I know you, don't I? Yes, you're the one Elena often talks about. Castillo, something.*

Sebastian reached out, but it was difficult, like he was neck-deep in black sludge. Even his thoughts were sluggish.

The hare fell back on its front legs and flattened its ears to its back.

He's coming.

Then, before Sebastian could call out, ask the hare to stay with him, it hopped back into the mist and vanished.

Elena.

Finally, he managed a thought, and with it, an image of her face flashed in his mind. Had she escaped, or was she at the mercy of the creature holding him hostage?

The mist parted again, but this time it wasn't the hare that stepped out but a teenager dressed in a graphic

T-shirt and ripped jeans.

Edward.

"Look at you," his brother said with a sneer. "Pathetic. I thought you, at least, would give me a challenge, but no. You were just as easy as the others." He rolled his eyes. "I hope Elena has more fight in her, or this is going to be one seriously boring day."

No! His thoughts slowly ramped up, fed by his anger and confusion. *It was you.*

Edward put his hands on his hips. "You're going to have to be a little more specific, my dear brother."

You killed Chloe.

Edward grinned. "Oh, yes, that was me."

Why?

"You know our sister, like a bitch with a bone." Edward scowled. "But that's enough from you. I don't want to be late for the main event."

Edward!

Again, it was too late. His brother vanished into the swirling clouds, leaving Sebastian alone with his thoughts.

****

After Sebastian left with the ice bucket, Elena laid out on her back and savored the warmth in her heart and the butterflies swirling in her stomach. Once they figured out the murder, she'd put real effort into their new relationship.

She peeked beneath her clothes at the snout of the boa, remembering how Chloe had possessed her without expelling her consciousness. If she could harness that, maybe the shades could help find the killer.

She shrugged out of her sweater, then concentrated. Instead of keeping herself protected, she expanded her mind to every flicker of shade nearby. Given that they were in a hotel, there were a lot of them, shining like thousands of stars.

She opened her eyes.

Shades formed on her skin, some done in a loose watercolor style, others in a traditional Japanese flowing pattern. The one thing they had in common was an utter lack of movement. Each stared up at her as if waiting for a response.

They were waiting for this. They wanted to help but couldn't until I asked.

Goosebumps spread up her arms. Despite the activity of the past few days, her body thrummed with energy. She took a steadying breath. What she was preparing to do was dangerous, even life-threatening. The shades might take control, drive her to madness, or kill her outright. But she needed them.

She used her most authoritative voice. "Do you understand me?"

The shades buzzed in place.

"I know we haven't been on the best of terms," she said. "But I'm asking for help. There's a shade that wants to kill me. A powerful one. I need your help to fight it."

She examined them one by one. The small snail by her elbow, its shell an intricate design of triangles. A dog of a breed she couldn't recognize sitting by her wrist lines crisp and sharp. The detail on his collar standing out to her, an alligator fabric. Many more littered her arms and chest. "There must be something you want from me. Whatever it is, I'll do it. Just help me."

Silence. She feared the shades would refuse or reject her offer. Then, between one breath and the next, they vanished.

She slipped her sweater back on and hoped the shades would find their target.

Then her phone started vibrating from her pocket, and she reached for it. When she didn't recognize the number, she rejected the call and tossed her phone on the table. The back of her head pounded.

"Sebastian," she called. "You back there?"

There was no response.

Her phone vibrated again, making a loud noise as it rotated around the table. Elena shoved it into her pocket. Whoever it was, they could call her as many times as they wanted. She didn't have to answer. She rolled off the couch and checked the bathroom for painkillers. When she found nothing, she walked through the connecting door to the other room, where the ice bucket lay on the ground. Ice spilled out of its mouth and onto the floor.

That's weird.

She exited the room and walked a few feet to the ice machine, but there was no sign of Sebastian. She looked up and down the hallway. There weren't any housekeeping carts.

Her phone rang.

Filled with a sense of urgency she didn't fully understand, she fished out her phone and pressed accept.

"Elena!" Sebastian cried through the phone. "Don't do anything he—" There was the sound of a scuffle, then a distorted voice said, "Cain house, one hour, or your boyfriend dies."

Click

****

Elena clutched her phone as she paced the suite.

"Please pick up, please pick up."

The line rang without connecting, and after the fourth attempt, she slammed her phone down on the table with a cry.

What the hell am I going to do?

The Harvester had almost won the last time they'd fought. It had only been her anger and desperation to keep Sebastian from being hurt that had given her the boost she needed. The odds of pulling that off a second time were slim. But she couldn't just let the monster do whatever he wanted to Sebastian.

She picked up the phone again, staring at it for several long minutes before dialing a number. It was a long shot, but she was desperate.

"Stillwood police," Sandra started before Elena cut her off.

"I need your help."

"Elena!" The sound of papers shuffling. "What's wrong?"

"I—Well…"

They record these calls.

"I understand," Sandra said. "Can I call you back at this number?"

She blew out a sigh of relief. "Yes."

Sandra hung up, and Elena cupped her phone in her hands, staring at it until it began vibrating again. She accepted.

"Okay, lay it on me," Sandra said.

Elena licked her lips. *A serial killer kidnapped Sebastian, and I need your help to get him back.* Was that too much? Would Sandra go off and tell Roth or her father? Maybe involving someone else was a bad idea.

"Is this about the case? Did you find something?"

"Not yet. We were getting ready to come up with a

plan when Sebastian was—well, he—I think the killer took him."

A beat of silence. "Did a ghost tell you?"

Elena had to swallow before she found her words again. "How do you know about that?"

A snort. "Girl, you're not the only one who is gifted around here. Those fools at Haven have been trying to recruit me for years."

She already knows. Oh, thank God.

She quickly filled Sandra in on everything that had happened since they had left her place. "Then my phone rang, and it was Sebastian, telling me not to come after him. So, it must be—"

"A trap, obviously." A gusty sigh. "You've sure had some fun without me, haven't you? Okay, you head over to the house and confront this bad boy. I'll be right behind you, and I'll bring the cavalry with me."

****

The wind ruffled Elena's hair, spreading it out behind her like a black cloud against the landscape of trees surrounding the house. She gathered it up and shoved it under a woolen cap.

Per Sandra's instructions, she'd waited as long as she dared before taking a very expensive cab out of the city. Her driver, a sweet old Black man, had questioned her choice of being dropped off at such a remote location, but she'd tipped him extra and promised she knew what she was doing.

If only I really did.

Courage faltering, she walked on, breath forming clouds of frost.

The porch of her childhood home was dark, creating an area hidden from the view of the house. If the perpetrator was waiting for her, they'd be there. The spot provided the most likely area for an ambush. It went against her better instincts, and she had to force her feet to continue moving.

"Hello?"

She concentrated on the crunch of dead leaves and scraps of wood beneath her feet.

A pile of rocks sat beside the porch. She tensed as she passed them.

Please don't let me down, Sandra.

Going into the situation without any real plan filled her with anxiety, but she pushed forward. She fought an internal struggle to remain calm, keeping her head high.

She climbed up the porch and unlocked the door.

A cold object pressed up against her scalp. She heard a click, like the safety of a gun being turned off. She jerked to a stop, then turned her head slightly so she could see her attacker's face.

Goose flesh prickled up her arms. "Hello, David."

"Hello, dearest," the creature inhabiting her lawyer replied. "It seems our little game is finally over."

"If you say so," she replied.

"Well, as nice as it is to see you again," David said. "I'm going to have to ask you to keep moving. We're on a schedule, you see."

She opened the door, and David followed, keeping the object pressed against her skull. She struggled to keep her calm.

"Stop there," David said.

She turned, expecting to stare down the barrel of a gun, but it was only a flashlight. The plaintive hooting of an owl sounded in the distance; the door was still open.

Now!

She yanked the stun gun from her pocket and slammed it into David's neck. She expected him to collapse, but he batted away the weapon as if it bothered him no more than a mosquito bite.

"Please," he said disparagingly. "Do you know how long I've been doing this? It would take something a lot more powerful to take me out, dearest."

So much for that.

She shuffled back and glared at him. "What have you done with Sebastian?"

David smirked. "Oh, don't worry about him. He's enjoying a long nap in your favorite place." He gestured with his flashlight to the hallway closet. She glanced at it, then back at David, before shoving past him and up the stairs, then throwing open the door.

It was empty.

From behind her, David burst into laughter.

She whipped around and charged him, determined to do whatever it took to get Sebastian back. But before she could make it halfway across the room, he drew a gun out from behind his back and pointed it at her.

She froze.

"Not quite my style, I know," David said. He tossed the flashlight aside. "As they say, get with the times. I think we both agree my approach has been less than successful."

She glared at him. "Where is he?"

David walked backward into the kitchen, then opened the pantry door with the hand not holding the gun. Sebastian fell out, smacking his head against the floor. There was duct tape across his mouth, and heavy rope wrapped around his body from his shoulders to his waist.

"Sebastian!" She jerked forward, one hand stretched out, but stopped when David shook his gun.

Please let him be okay.

She scanned every inch of him for injury. His eyes were closed, his face covered in scratches.

"He wasn't much fun," David said. "What a waste of time."

The blood rushed from her face, and the world blurred. She kept her arms raised and was careful not to move, not to provoke him.

"I don't understand," her voice broke. "Why not just take me? I know you can. You've done it before."

David grinned. "See, that was my original plan. Then you led me here, and I discovered something better. An entire group of you, like a buffet just for me." He licked his lips. "I thought I'd found my way in, then that brat confronted me. She refused to help me find Haven."

Her mind whirled. "It was you. You killed Chloe."

David grinned. "Guilty."

A flicker of white on his chest below the jacket caught her eye. A snowy rabbit peeked at her. She took it as a sign there was some part of David's soul left.

It took a significant effort to keep her voice neutral. "You can't kill me."

He laughed and gave her a horrifying mockery of a smile. "Why not? This town is like a circus. I don't know what the hell you're thinking, gathering like this. It makes it so much easier to pick you off, one by one." He grinned. "How about this? Get me into Haven, and I'll let you go. Once I have all those delicious souls, I won't need you."

Her heart pounded, adrenaline pumping through her veins. He offered her another chance at life. If she left, he would wait until she was too far to notify Haven, then mount his attack. But what did she owe them, anyway? They'd sat by and allowed dozens of others to die.

"Well? What do you say?" David took a step closer.

"Give me a minute to think about it."

What was there to think about? They wanted to cut her wings, keep her locked away. Maybe the world would be better off without them.

In a split second, Elena's life unfolded before her like an origami crane. If she took that path, many would suffer. She'd never see Sebastian and Sandra again. She might live another month, another year, maybe even another decade before the shades sent her to her grave, every moment spent on the run. Was a life of constant fear worth living?

With a start, she realized she'd made the choice once before. In choosing to run from Stillwood, she'd hurt Sebastian and Chloe.

She wouldn't make the same mistake again.

"No. I won't run away."

Chapter 19

David took two steps forward and thrust the gun against her temple. She breathed in the acrid stink of alcohol and sweat, felt the cool metal against her skin. The sensation honed her reflexes to a razor's edge. She thought she could predict how David would react. The shaking of the object in his hands was evidence the man she knew was still there somewhere.

"Listen," she said, keeping her voice calm. "You can take me. I won't resist. But only if you promise to leave Sebastian alone."

David snorted, but the gun shook harder. Her words were making an impact

"No!" David shouted. "One isn't enough." As he spoke, his voice changed, deepening to a rumbling baritone.

She met his eyes, and knowledge passed between them.

"Who are you? No, that's not right. Who *were* you?"

The shade possessing David's body laughed. "You've figured it out, have you? Like mother, like daughter. She took my life, and now I'll take yours."

Elena's heart dropped into her stomach. "Edward?"

It didn't make sense. The python on Sebastian's shoulders was Edward. Chloe had told her.

"Don't call me that," David snarled. "I cut that pathetic creature out of me."

Her stomach churned, and there was a sour-sick tang at the back of her throat. "You're the one who has been hunting me all this time? You killed Chloe? Your own sister?"

David's jaw twitched. "Bitch thought she could change my mind. Threatened to report me. And since you're not interested in helping me take down the others, I'll have you as an appetizer."

All along, she'd assumed the Harvester was the same shade that had taken over her mother. But it had been Edward who had formed as a shade and chased her all over the country.

"You don't have to do this," she cried. Fear squeezed her in its claws, and terrible images entered her mind. The things he could do with her body. The people he could hurt by pretending to be her. Everyone she knew would be at risk.

David took a step, forcing her to shuffle backward. That's when she noticed two other people in the house.

The first was Sebastian's friend, the one she'd met at the diner doing the food challenge. He met her gaze and held a finger to his lips, then pointed to the woman standing beside him.

It was Sandra, her arms splayed, her head tilted upward, her mouth open. Electricity sparked over her skin and gathered in her hands.

Elena stared, transfixed, until Peter waved his arm and mouthed the words "stall him."

Whatever she's doing, she needs time.

She forced her gaze back to David, who had his eyes narrowed. If she didn't do something, he'd turn around and see her friends.

Get him angry, and focused on you. What does he

hate more than anything?

"You know, it's a good thing we're ending our game now," she said. "You are so predictable. It was getting boring."

It worked. The suspicion fled David's face, and he bared his teeth. "Boring? Predictable? Impossible."

The flickering balls of energy in Sandra's hands grew to the size of apples. Was that enough?

Best keep going.

The more the Harvester focused on her, the better Sandra's chances of finishing whatever she had planned.

"Oh, yeah," she continued. "I can read you like a book. You're in it for the thrill of the chase. Now that it's over, you've lost interest. So predictable."

"We'll see about that," David said. Then he lunged toward her.

"Now!" Peter shouted.

David fell to the ground and flopped around as if he'd been hit with a bolt of lightning. At the same time, Sandra collapsed into Peter's arms.

"I'll take care of her," Peter called, hefting Sandra as if she weighed nothing. "You deal with that one. I don't think he's done yet." Then he exited out through the open sliding glass door to the deck.

They were right, of course, and she barely had a second to scuttle backward before David pushed to his feet. But the attack had done a measure against him. The veins on his face stood out in startling detail, and blood flowed from his nose and dripped down his chin.

"You bitch! I was planning on doing this nice and easy, but now you've tipped my hand." His face split in a wicked grin. "This is going to hurt."

He said something in a language she didn't

recognize, and a fierce, throbbing pain ripped up her arms. It was agony, like having her bones shattered one at a time.

The shade exerted its will over her, compressing her consciousness and forcing her to retreat deep inside her mind. So deep, she could no longer see or hear anything happening in the real world.

It's over. I did everything I could, and I still lost.

Her heart ached for Sebastian, Sandra, Peter. Everyone she knew. The Harvester would systematically destroy each of them for trying to stop him.

And on top of all that, the shades she'd hoped would help her had never appeared.

I wish I'd never had this curse.

Then, in the darkness, a flickering form appeared. First it was a man, then it morphed into the shape of a large cat, an eagle, and back to a man.

Who are you? What are you doing in my mind?

We have always been here.

The voice was a chorus of noises, speaking all at once. Male, female, young, old, human, animal. It was everything and nothing.

What do you want?

We have passed judgment.

It approached, and her mind exploded with static, like an old TV turned on to the wrong station, the noise echoing with a ferocity that sent her reeling.

Stop, please!

The pressure ebbed, and she sensed the creature was fighting with itself. She shrank from it, searching the darkness for some escape. What could she do to get it to leave?

You are unworthy of the gift, the creature finally

said. *But it is tied to your life force. We cannot take one without the other.*

The truth thrummed through her like a hammer blow. They wanted to kill her. Although at one time she would've gladly accepted death, faced with the prospect, she balked. There were so many people she didn't want to let go.

Please, I don't want to die. I promise I will no longer resist. Just don't kill me.

A mumbling all around her, a sense of disagreement, compromise, decision.

We agree.

The man melted away, and with it, the pressure on her chest dissipated. She expanded her mind to fill the vacant space. Inch by inch, she returned to herself, her feet, her arms, her nose.

She opened her eyes to see David's contorted face inches from hers, his features twisted into a mask of rage. "No! How did you resist?" He shook her, spittle flying from his lips. "How?"

A prickling started in her chest and spread to her arms, where the fox bounded through her skin. It reached David's hand and, with an audible popping noise, transferred into David's skin.

"No!" David scratched at his skin, dropping the gun. "No, go away!"

The fox prowled until it found its quarry. It pounced, struck the hare, and dug its teeth into the hare's neck.

Words whispered in her mind. *The soul has separated from the host. The transition is incomplete. Soon, the soul will die, and only the Harvester will remain.*

"Can you cure it?" Elena asked aloud. "Can you

help him? He wasn't always like this."

I can. It is what I am. It is what I do.

Without waiting for her to respond, the fox flexed her claws into the hare. It struggled for only a few seconds before David slumped to the ground.

Elena touched his body, and the fox climbed back onto her skin.

You have realized your purpose. You requested an exchange. This is what we ask of you. Seek the broken, the sick, and together we will heal them.

The fox winked at her before scurrying out of sight, leaving David's body unharmed but for a sheen of sweat over his skin.

With the danger dealt with, she scrambled into the kitchen and used a knife from the drawer to cut the restraints binding Sebastian, then carefully peeled the duct tape off his mouth. Although he was still unresponsive, the python graced his neck. A good sign. Edward, or whoever the python was, hadn't abandoned him.

"Ugh." The man in her arms stirred. "Elena?" He jerked upright. "Your lawyer. David. Where is he?"

She wrapped her arms around his neck with a half-sob, half-laugh. "He's dealt with. But it wasn't really David. It was Edward."

Sebastian squeezed her. "I know. I talked to him. He killed Chloe."

She melted into his embrace.

Then the sound of tires on gravel had her heart pounding once more. They got up and looked out the front window. A sleek, black limo idled in the driveway. The passenger door opened, and Aunt Martha stepped out, dressed in the same flowing robes she'd been wearing at Haven.

"Wait here," Elena said, stopping Sebastian from following. "I have to do this on my own." She made her way down the stairs, dreading the inevitable confrontation. She stopped a few feet from the car, out of grabbing distance, and folded her arms over her chest.

"Is it done?" Martha asked.

"It's done."

Martha's shoulders slumped. "Thank God." Then she smiled and walked forward, her arms outstretched. "I knew you could do it."

Elena backed up until her heel hit the steps. "What will happen to David?"

Her aunt shrugged. "I don't know. But I think he will sleep for a while, and when he wakes up, he will no longer be the man he was."

I hope he doesn't remember any of it.

Given what Edward had done while possessing his body, she suspected David would not want to have those memories back.

"Come, dear," Martha said, beckoning with her hands. "Let's go home. The council will let you stay now that the threat is dealt with. I made sure your room was prepared."

Elena remembered the stark white room with its pristine walls. Then she shook her head. "No. I'm staying."

Martha's smile faded. "You're sure?"

Elena looked up at the house. Sebastian stood in the window, watching her. "I'm sure."

Chapter 20

Elena navigated the Mini Cooper through meandering turns. The black stripes on the hood stood out against the snow on either side of the road. The windshield wipers passed back and forth, pushing great flakes of snow to the side of the car. It was shaping up to be quite the blizzard. The car drifted to the right. Her knuckles were white on the steering wheel, her back stiff from hours of driving half the speed limit on precariously icy highways.

She pulled up to the house, tires silent on the fresh concrete. The house had come a long way since she'd first come home so many months ago. Where once there had been a slate roof full of holes, the new metal roof glinted in the sun. Gone was the porch railing, half-rotted through. A metal railing stood in its place, identical in appearance but much sturdier.

She pushed the car door shut and trudged through the heavy snow drifts, vowing to buy a shovel on her next outing.

I'm actually staying in one place long enough to need a shovel.

The novelty still hadn't worn off on her, even after months of extensive renovations financed by the council at Haven. They'd been skeptical at first, but after she'd spent hours answering their questions and detailing her plans, they'd agreed to put up the money.

She'd made a deal with the shades, and she intended to honor it.

She took a step, and the ground shifted, her right foot sinking too far, disrupting her balance. She tugged, but her leg stuck firm.

Bloody Minnesota winters.

She tugged her foot and lurched forward as it sprang free without her boot. Resolving to find it later, she continued her route to the house, kicking through the snow with one freezing foot.

When she reached the porch, the door was open. Sandra stood in the doorway, her hands on her hips. "Lost another one, did you? It's going to be a minefield out there come spring."

"Very funny," Elena responded. She limped up the stairs and pushed past her friend and newest employee to enter the new headquarters of The Cain School for the Gifted.

She kicked her remaining snow-caked boot onto the mat by the door and then walked over to crouch by the crackling fire in the new fireplace. It had cost a bundle, but she had insisted upon it. The house was so remote that when the electricity flickered out, it was often out for hours, and she did not want future students to freeze.

So long as we have a place to store wood.

A lack of space was the crux of their current problem. The main floor retained the original kitchen and living space for communal use, and the rooms on the second floor had been converted into three double-occupancy dormitories with en-suite bathrooms. That left one major gap in their plans. They needed a classroom.

She thought of Haven, all those gifted individuals

trapped underground, their wings clipped. It pained her to think of them spending another six months in confinement.

The sooner we can get the school open, the better.

She peeled off her wet socks and draped them over the electric drying rack set by the fireplace, then flicked it on. When nothing happened, she unplugged it from the wall and plugged it back in. Still nothing.

"Let me," Sandra said. She hovered her hand above the fan, and three blindingly white miniature lightning bolts shot from her palm into the metal. The red light on the machine flickered on, and the fan started up with a mechanical whirring.

"What's wrong with it?" Elena asked. Their budget was already so tight, she didn't want to have to replace anything else. Parting with the fan would be especially tough, given how often she soaked her socks.

Sandra kept her hand held over the metal and released a few more lightning bolts. This time, the flickering streaks entered the machine for only a second before returning to Sandra's palm.

"Just a blown breaker," she said, rubbing her now-singed hand. "No big deal. I'll call Peter and ask him to pick up a replacement on his way in."

A blush spread across Sandra's face. Elena couldn't fight the grin spreading across her face. "How are things going on that front? You ask him out yet?"

Sandra's cheeks reddened further. "No. It's too soon. Janet is—I mean, his wife. She's—uh." She shrugged. "He's still married, you know. It's too soon, I think."

Elena hoped for Sandra's sake that Peter wouldn't pine for his missing wife much longer. From what she'd heard, the woman had been a complete tyrant, and her recent disappearing act was more of a blessing than anything.

From the next room, a male voice called out, "Elena? Is that you?"

"Yes," she called. "Wait there, I'll come to you."

She padded down the hallway on her bare feet into the tiny office they'd set up. David was inside, stapling a stack of papers together on a large wooden desk. His hands still trembled, and he had to walk with a cane some days, but he'd recovered since the attack.

"You are all set. For the record, I love what you've done with the place." He slid the papers into a large yellow envelope and handed it to her.

She accepted the envelope with a smile. "It was hard work, and there is much more work still to do. But progress continues. Thank you."

"You shouldn't be thanking me," David said as he stood from his chair. "Your real estate agent did all the hard work."

There was a creak from the other room, and then the thud of the outer door closing. She raced out of the room and back to the main foyer to see a tall man dressed in a heavy parka dusted with snow.

"Sorry I'm late," Sebastian said, grinning.

Elena's heart exploded into a swarm of butterflies the same way it did every time when she looked at her husband. He shrugged off his winter gear and then opened his arms in invitation. She flew into his embrace, wrapping her arms around him.

"I couldn't stop thinking about you," Sebastian murmured into her hair. "It's like we've been apart for years."

Elena laughed. "It's been hours!"

Sebastian feathered kisses down her neck. "It felt like years." Then he squeezed her tighter. "Are there any rooms we haven't christened yet?"

Her pulse hammered with anticipation at those words, and dampness gathered between her thighs.

"The office," she whispered. "Sandra just installed a lock this morning."

Giggling like teenagers, they hurried to the now-empty office. Elena sat on top of the desk while Sebastian locked the door. Then he turned to face her, a wicked grin on his face.

"There's something I've always wanted to try," Sebastian said. He shrugged off his shirt and tossed it into the corner. His finely sculpted chest was dusted with dark hairs that trailed down his abdomen and vanished beneath his pants.

"I'm up for something new," Elena replied. That was one of the things she loved about him, his curiosity and willingness to explore new techniques.

He stepped closer, and she hopped off the desk to meet him in a searing kiss, their tongues tangling in a slow dance. He tasted like caramel and apples, and the coarse stubble rubbing her cheek sent heat pulsing to her core.

He slipped his hands under the hem of her top, then up her sides, until it looped around her wrists. He formed a knot in the fabric, then dropped to his knees and trailed a line of hot, open-mouthed kisses from her navel up to the edge of her bra. He hooked his thumbs into her waistband and removed her pants and panties at the same time.

"This seems unfair," she said, eyeing the prominent

bulge in his jeans. "It's your turn, now."

He unzipped his fly and released his erect cock, stroking it twice before removing his jeans and boxers entirely. Their discarded clothing formed a heap in the corner.

"Turn around and put your hands on the desk," he said, his voice husky.

She did so, spreading her legs and raising her rear as if she was being frisked. If he was going to take the lead, she wasn't going to make it easy on him.

His cool hands circled her ankles, then massaged her shins and thighs before pausing to squeeze her hips.

"More," she said. His touch warmed her skin and made her tingle all over.

He leaned over her and cupped her breasts. The hard length of him pressed between her legs, nudging but not entering.

"Please." She gasped. Her whole body thrummed with pleasure, and wetness dripped down her thighs.

He unlatched her bra and pushed it to join her hands on the desk, then splayed his palm on her back and rocked back and forth, rubbing her entrance with the head of his cock.

"What do you want?" he asked. "Tell me."

"I want you inside me." She groaned. Her cheeks were so hot and pulsing with the rapid beat of her heart.

He slid into her sheath, inch by torturous inch. Then he waited, hard and throbbing inside her.

"What now?" He leaned forward to fondle her breasts again. His fingers tweaked her nipples, and she jerked at the sharp sensation, making him slide partially out.

Oh, I see.

She did it twice more before he cursed and began to thrust. The wet slap of their bodies was an intense sound, and she squeezed the muscles in her pelvis, seeking the thread of pleasure that would send her over the cliff.

Fingers touched her, and she moaned. He slowed his thrusts to a steady in and out as if he knew exactly what she liked best, and it wasn't long before the coiled pressure inside her released. She rode the orgasm until it faded, then jumped on the desk to spare her wobbly legs.

"That was amazing," she said, between panting breaths.

"I aim to please," he said. His cock was at full attention, bright red and beaded with a milky liquid. She marveled at his restraint.

"Round two?" she spread her legs wide.

He stepped closer, and she wrapped her arms around his neck, meeting his lips as he speared her, then rocked gently up and down. Her second orgasm was completely different from her first, gently fluttering up from the space where their bodies met.

His breath tickled her neck, and she giggled. He touched the tip of his index finger to her collarbone. "I like the new addition."

Elena smiled. She'd come up with a story, claiming it was a birthmark. Just between her breasts, a white pawprint was visible, as if a large cat had pressed her down.

A word about the author...

Melissa Kendall is a technical writer living in the windswept Canadian prairies with her two cats, Ella and Portage. You can find her on Twitter as @MAKendallAuthor. http://melissakendall.ca